empathy

KER DUKEY

Empathy
Copyright © 2014 Ker Dukey
All rights reserved. No part of this book may be reproduced or transmitted in any form without written permission of the Author.
This book is the work of fiction any resemblance to any person alive or dead is purely coincidental. The characters and story are created from the Author's imagination

Formatting by Champagne Formats

ISBN-13: 978-1500233396
ISBN-10: 1500233390

Other Books

The Broken Series
**THE BROKEN
THE BROKEN PARTS OF US**

My Soul Keeper

The Bad Blood Series
The Beats in Rift

Dedication

For the people who **LIVE**, despite how cruel the world can be at times.
Life has many roads, detours are inevitable. Some seek the road of righteousness. Some get lost down the path of sin, others run down it. Every now and then you find the path of redemption. Some paths are chosen for us but it's our freewill if we choose to follow it.

Preface

Blake

MY BIRTH NAME IS DAMIAN. Fitting, really, or so I'm told by the woman who named me.

"You're the devil's son," she would spit at me, pointing a shaky finger in my cheek in a drug induced haze whenever I refused to bend to her whim. I can still feel the impression of her fingertip where her nail broke the skin. I go by Blake now; it's my middle name, chosen by the midwife who brought me back from the dead. My mother couldn't wait for me to be out of her womb, expelling me too early from her body with the cord wrapped neatly around my neck, almost robbing me of the life I'd been gifted by a drunken fondle in the back of a truck.

They say some people are born with decreased activity in the brain; a cold spot in the front central lobe. Where most people have activity, a hot area giving them feelings, emotions and enabling them to love, there are a rare few who have a cold spot, affecting their ability to feel emotions, *empathy*. There are theories that serial killers have this cold spot. Psychopaths. That's why they lack the ability to connect, to care.

I don't have feelings the way most people do. I may be one of those people/psychopaths. I don't know. What I do know is I can fuck the woman who claims to love me and leave her before the sweat's even dried on my skin, knowing she will cry herself to sleep. I can supply my mother with cash to fund her drug habit, hoping this will be the final hit to send her to the afterlife *and*... I can kill without remorse.

My emotions are corrupted, have been since my life changed in a single night. My ability to give a shit is absent. I don't care about anyone with the exception of my kid brother, who is the sole reason I became a killer to begin with. Maybe I would have killed no matter what. Some people are born predestined to become evil, to mark the world with their darkness. Some paint the world in techno color, I paint it in red; blood red.

Can circumstances change us? Can the evil doings of others force us to change the path we're on? To alter the warmth in our souls? Can they dim our light, making us cold, dark, evil? I don't know. I've questioned this before, but now I accept this is who I am. Just like we cannot choose when the sun will rise and when it will set, I could not choose my destiny. It was mapped out for me. When life drowns you in its cruelty, you don't know which way the current will drag you, or who you'll be once you re-surface.

What I do know is, my emotions switched off when I came home from a party at eighteen years old, fully expecting a beat down by my Step father for coming home drunk after telling him I wouldn't be home that night. Instead I found him in my eleven-year-old brother's bed. I literally felt myself change. A flick of a switch. If there ever was a warm spot, it turned cold in that moment with the rest of me. Reasoning became impossible, questions I never thought I would have to ask raped my once placid mind. Shutters came down inside me, closing over the windows to my soul, changing me forever.

The muffled cries of my brother, muted because his head was pushed into his pillow while his own flesh and blood, the man who created him, the man supposed to protect, love and cherish him was

empathy

naked above him, changed my direction in life; mine and Ryan's, creating my step father's fate in the process.

    I didn't even flinch when I walked up silently behind him. The drunken haze cleared, nothing but rage burned in my veins, a blood red fog clouding my vision. Rage wasn't an emotion in that moment, it was an entity grown from the darkest depths of my being, vibrating through my skin to be released. Nothing felt more right than allowing it to take control, seek retribution for the abuse we were born into, to let it consume the boy who once lived there, devouring any human part left of my soul.

    The darkness I harbored deep inside that we all have under the surface took control. I gripped his head, and with all the strength I had, I twisted until I heard the loud pop, click, snap, whatever you want to call the sound of his neck breaking, ending his life and shutting off his switch to the stained soul inside him.

    I dragged his warm, sweaty body away from my brother, out of his room, closing the door behind me. Alcohol and sweat seeped from his pores, assaulting my nose and making my stomach twist with more hate than I knew possible. I dropped him at the top of the stairs and nudged him with my foot. His lifeless body thumped down, landing in a heap at the bottom. The man who gave my brother life, who had been all I knew as a father figure was now nothing but a decomposing body. If I could have killed him again and again, I would have, without hesitation. I went to the shower and turned it on before going back to my brother's room and scooping up his trembling body. I put him on his feet, told him to shower and promised no one would ever hurt him again.

    When I called the police the next morning, telling them I got up to find my dad had an accident, they didn't question my story that he was a drunk, and no one cared enough to argue foul play. The reports said accidental death. Our father was well known for liking the bottle.

    Ryan and I moved in with our waste-of-life mother, and if it wouldn't have been suspicious for both our parents to have accidents in such a small time frame, I would have killed her too. Instead, I gave her money to disappear for days at a time until I turned twenty-two, finished my degree in criminal justice, joined the police force and got custody of Ryan. Then I paid her to disappear to distant relatives.

I took martial arts classes and shooting lessons after that night. I wanted to be able to protect my brother from any threat. I earned extra money through my computer skills to buy Ryan anything he needed and to support our mother's habit. Ever since I was little I knew computers. I can hack pretty much any network, and I used that skill to earn petty cash from students wanting grades changed, or finding information on people that was kept in confidential files. I worked solely through my computer; I couldn't risk my identity being compromised. To contact me you had to already know about me through word of mouth, then email one of my many accounts that would go into spam file I never opened, so if someone stumbled across that email account, it looked inactive on my part.

This system also worked for me when I became a contract killer. I can see the sender's email address without having to open the email. Just having that small piece of information, I can get into their emails, send viruses that clone their hard drives, giving me access to everything they do, which in turn gives me passwords to their accounts, including their online banking. I can find out every single thing about them and their life with one simple address, and if I find them trustworthy and wealthy enough to afford me, I bring up a chat box, scaring the shit out of them. I have two more chats with them before completing the job they want me for. Then I never speak to them again.

I have only a few rules:

One: Never do more than one job per client. Once they see how easy it is to get away with murder they tend to become a little kill happy. They would have me killing the neighbor for playing music too loud if they could.

Two: Never take a job close to home. When people use the term 'don't shit where you eat' well, I don't kill where I live. It just makes sense.

Three: No one knows who I am, my name, age, what I look like or if I'm even male; which is why everything is done through an untraceable computer.

I make a shit load for my services. I have to be clever not to flash

empathy

my cash, swapping my funds into offshore accounts and getting a normal job so I look like everyone else. That's why I joined the police force; who better to teach you how to kill and how to avoid being caught than the police?

My life course was chosen that night when I was eighteen, when I took a life and didn't feel remorse. When I overheard some rich college kid telling his friend he would pay a million for someone to kill his overbearing father, I knew he was talking hypothetically but I also knew there were people who would pay for someone to kill for them and right then, in that moment, my career path was chosen. It took me six months in the academy, training, three months field training, two years cut loose on patrol and I made detective at the tender age of twenty-five. I'm the youngest detective to ever be sworn in at our department but I'm good at my job. Just like they train me to be a better killer, who better to find criminals then a master criminal?

Chapter 1

Salutation

Melody

"MELODY." THE T.A ECHOES MY name as he sifts through a stack of papers on his desk. He grins up at me when he finds mine and hands it to me. "You write about music with so much passion. Appropriate, really, with your name."

I offer him a weak smile. The truth is, music is my mom's passion. I was taught piano and made to have vocal lessons to appease her but I want to go into journalism, do some good, and report real news.

I walk the steps to take my seat next to the guy who I now know as Ryan; it's scribbled on his paper with an A grade beside it. He always wears dark clothes and eludes interaction by never looking up from his notepad. I've attended creative writing for four weeks now and not once has he looked at me. I occasionally brush my leg with his, just to see if I can provoke any reaction from him. It never works. He's always so engrossed in whatever he's writing, as if the rest of the world doesn't exist. My curiosity to know what he writes when in that world of his has made me lean towards him on more than one occasion to steal a glimpse of what makes him worthy of those As, but I still receive no reaction, not even a *back off*.

A few assholes called him a freak on the first day, and then went on to talk about what they would do to me. *Wreck me,* I think they said. I thought college would be different from high school but it turns out the dynamics are pretty much the same.

My thoughts go to Zane. We dated through high school and he was popular for all the right reasons. He played sports and was intelligent. He had no time for bullies and gave everyone a chance. He was confident, outgoing and gorgeous. We had a puppy love, pure and beautiful. When we parted at the beginning of summer with a promise to always be friends it was a sad day, but a necessity. We were headed to different colleges after spending a year traveling together, temptation would be everywhere. He'll always have a special place in my heart. He was my first love, the boy I gave my virginity to, but it wasn't soul clenching, heart stopping love. We both deserve to have fun and then, later in life, find the love that devours everything that came before.

I rub the tattoo on my wrist. Zane used to call me his moonflower; "Queen of the Night," a species of cereus flower that only blooms at night. I'm not a morning person. I'm often late and grumpy and I only come back to life at night. Zane told me I blossom in the moonlight, and he took my innocence under the beam of the moonlight in the back of his pickup truck. Not romantic to most but it was perfect for us, and he carved a little bit of his identity into my soul that night.

A sigh leaves me, making me conscious of the fact I'm in class and not at home alone. I risk a look at Ryan, who luckily, remains true to his character, ignoring me. His eyes almost seem shut, like he's snoozing. I stroke the moonflower with LIVE tattooed underneath it. Zane and I got identical tattoos the day we parted, to remind ourselves to live. Life can be too short for some of us, a lesson he learned after his sister was the victim of a hit and run. Annabelle died at the scene, left in a ditch for three hours before she was found. If the car had stopped and got her to hospital she would still be here, breathing, going to school, falling in and out of love. Dreaming, aspiring to be the actress she wanted to become, to live a life beyond her short thirteen years. The same week, a celebrity who had passed through our town was getting married; guess which story got the front page?

I slip my paper into my bag without checking the grade and take out my tablet. I quickly check my emails while I wait for the class to fill. There's an email from my mother dated yesterday, reminding me she would like me to visit this weekend. Her and Daddy won't be happy I haven't replied. I check my phone, relieved but surprised I don't have a missed call or text from them. I read through the email. She's called a family meeting and wants me there, repeating the same information she told me a week ago. I involuntarily roll my eyes at the screen, knowing how much of a drama queen my mother can be. If I go all the way home just to be told she wants my opinion on drapes for her new study, I will scream. I'm already dreading the night drive. I left it too late to book a flight after insisting I didn't need Mom to do it for me. I close the email screen and look up at the T.A, Mr Walker, who hushes the class.

"There were some great pieces handed in for your first assignment." He looks at me and Ryan with a soft smile and a head tilt, making me blush when all eyes follow his.

"And then there were some that made me think you only took this class because you had no other choices." He frowns, looking over at the jock douches who take slouching more seriously than the class.

"For your next assignment I want you to partner up."

Ryan groans and yawns; it's the most vocal he has ever been. A small smile lifts my lips at his obvious dislike of interacting with something other than his pen.

"I want you to pick one thing one of you is really passionate about, discuss it in detail and then both write about it. I want to see how different the perspectives are from the person who is passionate about the subject and the partner who is indifferent about the subject."

I watch as the jock asshole in the front row stands and looks over the rows of seats; his eyes land on me. He walks towards the stairs, his

empathy

gaze never leaving my face. *Oh, God. No way am I teaming up with him.* I nudge Ryan harder than intended, making his pen slip and draw a line across his paper. I grimace when his eyes turn to me and squint; they're cold, like a black abyss.

"Sorry," I mouth, my nose wrinkling. My eyes widen as the Jock gets closer. Ryan notices him approaching and speaks up.

"She's partnering with me. Go find different prey."

The jock opens and closes his mouth for a minute before grunting his reply. "Why would she want to write about your passion? You're a depressed freak who probably cuts himself."

Hairs rise on the back of my neck and my stomach drops. What a narrow-minded, childish thing to say. I've felt a weird need to stick up for Ryan ever since the first day of class when I saw him sitting on his own with his face in his notepad. He's different, quiet and he does seem to only wear black but it's just jeans and a tee. He looks normal; not that someone who chooses to dress differently isn't normal, but he's better than normal. He has brown wavy hair, thick and mussed into a just-got-out-of-bed style. His dark brown eyes are oval shaped, and his lashes frame them perfectly, giving him an intense gaze. He has full lips and a strong jaw, a lean athletic build and he's easily six foot tall.

"And how did you come up with that assumption?" Ryan asks with honest curiosity, a grin on his face as he taps his pen on the table.

The jock laughs and points at him. "Look at you, always wearing black, never speaking or looking at anyone. You scream self-harmer." He smirks, obviously proud of his observation.

"Wow, your assessment should be written in a psychology text book. Seems you have it all figured out. *Or* you could be a stupid fuck whose mentality is still stuck in high school." Ryan shifts in his seat, leaning towards him, his tone confident. "I wear black because I happen to look good in black. I don't look at people often because when I do, chicks think I want to fuck them and guys think I want to fight them. I don't talk to people because it's rare I find anyone worth engaging in conversation."

I'm speechless and my eyes burn a hole in the side of Ryan's face. I can't look away. He's always seemed withdrawn and yet here he is, confident and bold.

"Everything okay here?" Mr Walker asks, walking up behind the jock whose fists are now clenched so tight his knuckles have paled and his eyes are burning into Ryan's.

"Everything is fine, Mr Walker, but I have to leave early today if that's okay?" I politely ask, drawing his attention to me.

"That's fine, Melody. I'll email you any notes you might miss out on today."

He turns and walks back to the front of class, quickly followed by the jock. I look to find Ryan's intense gaze on me. I smile and his eyes scan my face.

"Hi," he says, his voice deep, warm. I feel heat from the blush I know is tinting my cheeks.

"So, I'm worth engaging in conversation?" I raise an eyebrow.

One side of his mouth lifts into a half smile. "Well, I don't think we can do this assignment without talking, so I'm taking a chance that you might just have something worth saying. I'm very interested to know what you're passionate about, Melody."

The heat from my blush sets fire to my skin. "I'm free Sunday if that works for you?" I tell him, packing my iPad into my bag. I drag my eyes from his, getting to my feet.

He pulls out his cell and hands it to me. "Add your number."

I try to ignore the provocative picture of a woman naked and bound on her knees that is his screen saver but the image is graphic and not really something I expect to see as someone's screensaver that they willing hand over for people to add their numbers too. Regardless I choose not to judge him for his choice of image, and add my number before slipping his phone back to him.

I make my away from the class room without looking back, even though I'm dying to know if he's watching me.

The fresh summer air breezes over me, caressing my skin. The scent of fresh cut grass fires my senses, and memories flash of summers back home when I was a kid. My eyes are trained on my phone, sending a quick text to my mom to let her know I'm leaving soon and should be home by midnight, when I collide with a steel pillar, knocking me backwards to the ground. My bag drops from my shoulder and my phone flies in the direction of the bushes. I look up into the

empathy

penetrating gaze of the steel pillar, who happens to be a guy. I can't really make him out with the sun behind him but his brow furrows as he glares at me, telling me that colliding with him and me falling on *my* ass has inconvenienced him somehow.

He steps around me muttering, *"idiot"*, and not subtly. I don't know what possesses me but I jump to my feet, raising and swinging my bag as I do. I lash it right at him, hitting his retreating body with a thud. He turns fast, grabbing the bag and yanking it forward with me still attached to the handle. I fly towards him, crashing full force into his chest and crumbling to the floor onto my already sore ass.

I glare up at the tank. "What is your problem you…you…" My brain abandons me as I stutter, sounding as if I don't have the IQ to even be in college. "Fucking dick." I grimace at my total lack of maturity, wittiness and language. I'm not one to swear. *Fucking dick,* I repeat in my head, chastising myself.

"My problem is you running into me then attacking me with your bitch purse that weighs a freaking ton. Then throwing yourself at me and falling at my feet talking about fucking my dick."

I exhale the breath I sucked in at his description of what happened. "You must have malfunctioned when I bumped into you because you're clearly delusional. Oh, and don't offer to help me up or anything," I grumble, getting to my feet.

"I wasn't going to. You're clumsy and weak. You need to strengthen your body and look where you're going."

I flinch from his clear distaste for me, my mouth dropping open. I can't believe he said that. He doesn't give me time to formulate a witty comeback, he just walks away, leaving me seething. Damn, he is built. Anyone would fall on their ass running into that brick wall. The muscles in his back pull his t-shirt tight, showcasing them, and he has a firm ass. *Shit!* I reprimand myself. *He does not have a nice ass. He's a total jerk.*

I scramble for my phone and manage to make it to my car without any more incidents. She's a sleek BMW 4 series convertible; very *rich girl* but my father insisted I have it. He wanted me to have a new car when I started college so I wouldn't have to get rides from guys, or become stranded if I needed to come home. He hated the idea of me going to college so far away but after I went traveling with Zane, he accepted it. I'm his baby, his only daughter. I have a half-brother but he's never lived with us. He arrived before my mom stole my father's heart, and apparently, someone else's husband. I never knew this until I met my half-brother when I was eleven and he informed me my mom is a husband-thieving whore. My relationship with him has always been strained, so I ignore him for the most part. I'm not looking forward to this family meeting tomorrow knowing he'll be there.

I pull open my car door and smile at the two girls beaming at me as they walk past. I haven't really made any friends since I got here so it's nice to have a friendly smile in passing.

Chapter 2

Reaper

Melody

MY FIRST THREE HOURS ON the road pass in a haze of headlights and blurry scenery, my mind replaying my day. The fact Ryan actually spoke, and then the stranger who had no manners or people skills. *Who knocks someone on their ass and doesn't offer to help them up?*

I crank the radio louder as Paramore's *Now* fills the car, and refuse to think about the douche anymore. The fuel gauge catches my eye as I drum my fingers on the steering wheel, humming along before bursting out and hollering the lyrics, drowning out the smooth crooning from the speakers. The gauge blinks at me, forcing me to indicate when I spot a gas station.

The screen of my phone lights up with a text message. It has no name but I know straight away it's from Ryan.

So, the guy from class found his passion. It happens to be aggression towards my pretty face. His name is Clive btw. I may not speak much in class but I do pay attention to my surroundings.

My anger spikes at the idea of the jock hitting Ryan. After adding Ryan's name to the number, I hit save and slip my phone back in my bag. I hate gas stations at night; they're eerie despite the lights illuminating the pumps.

The cool breeze nips at my arms, making me shiver as I exit my warm, safe car. Yawning, I pump the gas until the tank is full then go inside to grab a Red Bull to keep me alert for the rest of the drive.

"Is that all?" I look up into the brown eyes of the cashier; he has broad shoulders, a strong jaw and a shaved head. He keeps licking his lips at me, making me feel like I'm on display.

"And gas." I point to my car, the only one in the lot.

He smirks at me, his eyes lingering on my chest while he gives me my total. *God, has he never seen a woman before? What is it with guys being total jerks today?*

"Hey!" I click my fingers in his face to bring his pervy stare to my face. "This is a gas station not a strip joint. These…" I gesture to my chest, "…are not how I pay for my gas, so stop staring at them like they're going to spring from my top and dance on the counter!"

His eyes widen a fraction before he snatches my credit card out of my hand. I feel his eyes on me as I leave.

I will be taking a hot shower before crawling into bed when I get home.

I open my car door and slide into my seat, locking my doors, then grab my phone out of my bag to text Ryan back before setting off.

He hit you? How's the damage? M x

empathy

His reply is instant, making me smile.

Not bad. I told you I look good in black. Even with black eyes.

I hope you at least got a hit in. M x

Nope, I just let him hit me. He wants to make assumptions about me, let him think I'm a freak.

I can imagine his mind working overtime trying to work out why you didn't fight back but he's so small minded he will still only come up with "because you're a freak". M x

I know and just to freak him out I'll wear the title with pride. You're a freak lover btw, according to Clive The Giver of Titles.

I'll wear it with pride. M x

I slip my phone away and spot the huge grin plastered on my face in the rear-view mirror. I like this Ryan guy. He's the first person I've met who I think I will enjoy being around since starting college.

Seven long, tiring hours in my car, only to break down a mile from our house. A grumble leaves me as I pull my overnight bag from the trunk and abandon my "safety net" car.

Walking for twenty minutes to get to our house in the dead of night, ignoring the high pitched call of grasshoppers shattering the night's silence is a chore.

Grass hoppers creep me out! One jumped down my dress once when I was little and traumatised me against them for the rest of my life.

Familiarity engulfs me when I rush up the drive. The huge white house is a beautiful structure sitting on its own, only surrounded by nature. I love it here, the smell of the fresh cut grass, the muggy heat sticking to my skin turning to chills when the occasional breeze wisps through the air and reminds me of the long summer nights of my youth.

The house has five bedrooms, and although only three of us live here, with Mom's touch, it still feels homely. Mom could have gone bigger with Daddy's wealth; I think she was quite tame when it came to buying this house. Daddy works in banking and made some lucrative investments, sky rocketing him to become a millionaire. He's country through and through, and the money never changed that, giving me the best of both words; wealth so we never had to worry, but also a down to earth, well-rounded daddy.

I moan at the darkness that awaits me; not one light left on. *Thanks, Mom.* Rummaging through my purse, my eyes already adjusting to darkness of the night, the only light is from the full moon casting a tinted blue glow. My fingers find my house keys and I sag in relief. I'm tired and just want to shower and slink in to my familiar bed, and wake to Mom's coffee and pancakes.

I start to insert the key but the door is slightly ajar, barely noticeable to anyone not trying to get in. *Mom must have left it open for me.* I slowly push the door further and a chill races up my spine. I'm tired but my brain has caught up with me. She wouldn't leave the door open, she knows I have a key. Intuition warns me not to go in but I shrug it off and tell myself I'm being stupid. Like most girls, I convince myself bad things won't happen to me. This is my family home, it's perfectly safe.

Lowering my overnight bag to the floor, I take a few small steps inside. It's quiet and dark, but it's late so that's normal. *Stop being paranoid, you're just tired.*

I walk to the console table and drop my keys down. They make a loud clanking sound, making me "shhh" them. My own image in the overhead mirror makes me squeal and jump a foot in the air. "Oh my

empathy

God, Mel. Get a grip."

It happens so quickly, like a cloud passing in front of the sun, a flash of lightning in a storm, a shooting star in the black night sky. A shadow crosses the mirror before a hand grips my throat. The cold leather of a gloved hand as it encases my life in its palm brings disbelief followed by a sheer dread I'd never experienced before. Fear solidifies my blood. *"This isn't real, this isn't real,"* echoes on repeat in my mind.

A warm body pushes up against my back. Mint scent from his breath wisps against my ear, dispersing down my cheek and invading my nose. A whimper escapes my lips and I reach up to pull away the hand gripping my throat, my survival instincts wanting to release the vice hindering my breathing.

The pressure eases with an audible gasp from his lips. The warmth from his body leaves my back momentarily as he takes a step away from me. Regaining his composure before I have a chance to act upon whatever spooked him, he reinforces his grip. I know it's a man from his strength and size. There's a hint of something from his scent clouding me, a strong soap… surgical soap.

I look into the mirror but I can't see him. He's behind me, in shadow, dropping his knees slightly so his face is covered by my head. The darkness of the lobby taunts me. Every child's nightmare will forever be my fear no matter what age I reach if I make it from here; shadows taking form from the darkness

Please be dreaming, Melody. This can't be real. This can't be real.

His grip is so tight, his hand nearly wraps around my entire throat. My eyes gloss over and a single tear leaks from my eye. I can't believe this is happening; is this really me? I feel like I'm watching someone else's nightmare play out through my eyes.

"Life is too short, Mel. I want you to live it." Zane's words mock me instead of comforting me.

The growl from my reaper drags me into the present. My throat is raw as I choke out my final words. Death is close; I feel it in the air. I walked into my tomb when I didn't listen to my instincts and stepped foot into this house.

"You fucking coward. At least face me if you're going to kill me," I rasp out, my last ounce of courage spilling from me. I won't die whimpering, this is what sickos get off on. He can't have that. I refuse.

He spins me around to face him so fast it leaves me dizzy. He's so strong I'm weightless in his grasp. I lift my gaze to meet the face of my killer but before our eyes connect my head is forced backwards. A sharp pain explodes against my head before my body goes limp and I succumb to the dark fog taking my vision.

My skull is cracking in two. Oh God, it's going too spilt right down the middle. Moaning, I reach up to hold my head.

I don't remember drinking or tackling a truck last night so why do I feel so bad? My fingers are met with a huge, seeping gash. I wince on contact.

I quickly become aware, bolting up and scanning the space around me to see if I'm alone. Silence. Stillness. I'm alone but that same eerie atmosphere lingers in the air.

I want to go back to the two seconds of not remembering. Fear ricochets from the pit of my stomach to every nerve ending, my skin covering me in goose bumps. I'm vibrating, my teeth tap dancing against each other from the force of my tremors. I have no idea how long I was laid here. Minutes? Hours?

The dark corners of the house look like a black void i can't make anything out. I need to turn on every light to expel the night. I check myself over for more injuries, making sure all my clothes are intact. I'm still fully dressed.

Pushing myself up, I flinch when the glass from the cracked mirror cuts into my palm.

"Argh," I croak, my throat raw, my voice unfamiliar to my own ears.

I stumble slightly once I get to my feet, and use the console table to steady myself.

"Mom! Dad!"

My brain screams at me, telling me to shut the hell up and get out

empathy

of here but I just want my mom and dad.

Venturing further into the house, the blood from my palm trickles, leaking down my fingers leaving a dripping path like the breadcrumbs trail from Hansel and Gretel, only this trial leads further into a nightmare, fitting that it be blood.

My heartbeat storms in my ears, making my head throb.

Thump.

Thump.

Thump.

Stop!

No heartbeat, no breathing, just silence, death, then my own wail and the thud from my knees hitting the hardwood floor. My bloody palm covers my open mouth. Silent screams rip at my insides, tears setting fire to my eyes.

"No, no, no, no, no, no," I mumble, placing my palms to the floor and crawling to my father's lifeless body. His eyes are open, staring at me, the jade green that match my own is gone. They look like a sheet of ice has frozen over them, distorting the color. His tanned skin is pale and papery.

"Daddy. Daddy, wake up. Please wake up."

I look over his body, the dark red stain spread across his shirt like a pattern on a tie dye skirt from the sixties. It's crazy, the things that enter your mind when nothing makes sense. I look for the wound that is letting his life escape from him, placing my hand over it, my jumbled mind trying to sift through the CPR I learnt in school. My hands are shaking so much I can't steady them.

He is dead; my palms can feel the cold, congealed ooze of his blood beneath them. That's when I notice the moistness under my knees. I scoot back like I've been electrocuted, my butt skimming across the room, kicking my legs forcibly against the wood to move me away faster, away from the nightmare I woke up in.

I rush to my feet and run towards the phone. That's when I see her. Her head is down; the blood covering her chest completely disguises the color of her top. Her dark hair is limp, falling into a plate of food set out in front of her. The rest of the table is a mess, there's food everywhere, and a bottle of wine has tipped over. She would be so mad at this mess.

I slowly walk towards her. "Mommy," I whisper, knowing she's dead, but the small girl that believed in fairies and Santa Claus has come to the surface. "Mommy, I'm home. Please wake up. Please wake up, Mommy. Mommy!"

I'm at least eight feet from her but her river of blood pooling beneath her chair is cutting of my path to her, more blood then I've ever seen; how can this much blood come from one person? Her skin is so pale. *Snow White,* the little girl taking hostage of my mind whispers.

I reach out to her. "Mommy." But she's not here anymore. There is nothing but tainted air and the shells of my butchered family.

Collapsing to the floor, I don't know how long I sit there but it feels like a lifetime. The scent from their decomposing bodies fills my nose, making me gag. The metallic taste from the blood in the air attacks my taste buds.

There's a buzz of noise around me, and the silhouette of a man fills my vision. I scream and try to push him away but I'm quickly restrained. I fight, screaming until I feel a sharp stab in my thigh. A numb reprieve seeps over me, blanketing me, protecting my frail splintering mind, and then… nothing.

Chapter 3

Intrigue

Ryan

I SIT THROUGH THE REST of class the way I always do. I'm there, for all intents and purposes, the genetic make-up of flesh and bone. My thoughts, however, left with Melody. Four weeks I've been coming to class. Four weeks I've managed not to molest her with my eyes or hands, even though my mind was working overtime, imagining her in every position possible but always reverting back to doggy style while I tug on that luscious mane of hair and fuck her hard and fast, slipping from her pussy that I know will be tight, to her ass which is probably still virginal. I want to know what noises she makes. Want to see how far I can push her. What would a princess like her let me do before telling me no?

I like the release of sex. There isn't much I find pleasure in and I don't really find pleasure in sex, but it's an outlet for me. I love pushing a person's thresholds. I love to degrade them. Sadistic? Yes.

Damn, I hope she likes it rough because my hand practically vibrates to spank that tight little ass of hers. I know I should stay away from her, that's why I ignored her when she decided to sit next to me. I'd noticed her amongst the crowds before we even got to class; her thick layers of chocolate hair that glimmer with specks of red in the sunlight, her green eyes shine bright even from a distance. Life and happiness dance in them. She is a blossomed rose in a vine of thorns. She stands out with her perfect womanly figure, round perky tits, a small waist, and hips that beg to be held on to, an ass that screams to be ridden and legs that go on for days, dying to be spread wide and cuffed to my bed posts.

I'm not the only one to notice her. Guys swarm around her like bees to honey. She must know how attractive she is but she plays it off, nonchalant. It intrigues me but after fucking every willing slut in high school and it causing nothing but drama and attention I didn't need, I decided I'll only fuck outside of my own college. My desired prey needs to be depraved like me so when I do spank her or surprise her with sex toys mid-fuck, she won't run away screaming or crying rape.

I don't care about the law but I take great pride in eluding them if I ever step over the line. I've labelled this pretty little thing, Melody, off limits, and she makes it hard, especially when her firm thigh brushes against mine, making my dick want to jump out of my pants straight into hers, testing her stamina in humiliation. I want to film me fucking her mouth, just to taunt her with the fact I have it. And even though I'm not going to indulge in my fantasies, fate has intervened. It's destined to happen so I embrace it and play along, the game set out too perfectly for me not to play.

She practically shines with the air of money. I saw a few of her texts when she didn't know I was watching, safety reminders or something from her dad. Warning her to charge her phone, carry her pepper spray, and lock up before she goes to sleep. An over-protective parent. God, she's from another world. I'm only here in college because I was

empathy

born bright. I have no clue where those genes come from but both Blake and I are talented, with well above average IQs. Blake also paid my full tuition and made me promise I would work hard and make a life for myself. He's convinced he won't always be around.

'*Some souls have a purpose, Ryan. Mine is to see you into adulthood and make sure you live and make something of yourself. You deserve to be happy and never feel anything but the good in the world.*'

Guilt is a powerful motivator. Guilt has moulded Blake's entire life. He never thinks about himself or what he deserves. I often study him, trying to crack into his mind to see how he sees things from our life. He committed the ultimate sin for me and that leaves a mark on someone. He thinks by shutting the world out, being anonymous to emotions, he has no conscience. But if guilt powers him, and memories of an ultimate betrayal fuel his blood, how can he be emotionless? I never mention this stuff to him, they're just thoughts I muse over when watching him.

I'm good at watching the world around me without people knowing I'm recording everything, storing it away to muse over later. People's actions, personalities, desires and actions fascinate me. I'm not delusional. I know I'm not your average young man. I give a *stay the fuck away from me* vibe on purpose. I have hard-to-satisfy urges and just because they're frowned upon doesn't mean I don't do them, it just means I have to be wittier than everyone else around me and, lucky for me, I am.

I grew up quickly. I was never shown affection, well except from Blake, and even then he was more screwed up then me so his affection wasn't the cuddles and good advice kind, it was more the *I'll buy you anything you want, I'll show you how to fight and I will kill for you* kind of affection.

Our mother is a cold-hearted whore who lets men fuck her for sport, and that's where I get my *women are usable fuck objects* views from. Our father was a drunk who assaulted Blake and me, completing my fucked up psyche. I didn't stand a chance of being normal, and because of my issues, I like to be beaten for fun. I like to go to dark, smutty clubs and let Doms or Dommes whip the shit out of me. I tell them it's to punish me for my father's abuse, for my mother not loving me and for my brother becoming who he is for me. The truth is I want them to whip some feeling into me, make me feel the guilt Blake lets consume him. When it doesn't work, just feeling the cursed blood inside me leak out as I taunt the Dom with my laughs at his attempts to hurt me gives me a little buzz, and I crave that buzz. I like pain, and pushing someone to inflict it is the only thing I gain satisfaction from.

Fuck. Clive the asshole in his cashmere golf club sweater is right. I am a freak and a self-harmer; accept I'm not the one doing the cutting. I let others cut into me instead.

Chapter 4

Pleasure in pain

Ryan

I LEAVE CLASS AND NOTICE that Clive and his *close* friend, Jacob, follow me. A sick part of me revels in the fact they'll try to hurt me but only give me pleasure. I push through the main doors, squinting from the change in light. Blake is across the green, propped up against a tree, his demeanour unapproachable. It makes me smirk how girls still stare and smile coyly in his direction. Fucking whores. I raise my hand slightly by my side to signal him to stay where he is. His eyes dart to Clive who shoves me from behind.

"Got nothing to say now your freak lover isn't here to hear you acting the big man?" Clive spits.

I turn to face him as he raises his arm and hits me with a closed fist right to my jaw. My tooth pierces the soft tissue and begins to bleed; the taste firing off all the dark places in my mind. I smile at him and laugh in my mind at his confusion.

"Come on, pussy. Are you not going to hit me back?" He hits me again, catching my eye, the pain exploding and giving me chills.

"Mmm, I'm going to fuck Melody in the ass and think of you when she squeals," I retort. My smile grows when he shakes his head as if he just imagined those words leaving my lips. I said it quietly enough that only he would hear them.

My pleasure doesn't last. Blake's fist comes from the right, quick as a flash, landing hard on Clive's face. He goes limp, collapsing to the floor like someone cut the strings from a puppet.

"I don't have time for you to get off, Ry. I need to be somewhere," Blake says, looking down at the guy he just knocked out.

I swipe the blood from my lip, sucking it from my thumb as I follow Blake to my car.

"Drop me at the airport. It's just a quick stop over. I'll be back tomorrow morning. I don't like having to come here to give you a simple message, Ry. I hate you spending the night in those clubs and I've told you to come home to crash, and keep your phone on so I can contact you."

I know not to ask questions when he needs to go out of town and it's meant to be kept between us if anyone asks, not that we have anyone who will ask. I know he worries if I don't come home but I don't care. I was busy feeding my urges last night.

I don't answer him, my mind on the fact he's s leaving. I blew my stash of cash last night. He always leaves me extra when he goes out of town, like a guilty bribe which pays for my night of pain. My mind is already in the club, tied to the rack, enjoying the bite of Mistress Dawn's Whip.

I drive on auto pilot and before I can blink I'm waving Blake off. I text Melody, establishing some form of relationship so she won't be shocked if I push for a little something from her on Sunday. I want to watch her unravel in every way, despite my first thoughts to stay away from her. I'm too fascinated by her now, and the coincidence of cir-

empathy

cumstance tells me it is meant to be, and anyway, she pushed the issue by making contact with me to provoke a reaction. What she doesn't realise is she got my attention weeks ago, and again when she giggled at one of those texts from her dad. Her laugh is so light and breathy, easy like the flapping of a bird's wings taking flight, effortless and graceful. Hmm, she has my attention and today played out perfectly.

    I go home to shower and then make my way to the club.

Chapter 5

Impact

Blake

I'VE NEVER HESITATED BEFORE. I kill without remorse. The girl who loves me, Abby, the one I fuck and leave because I don't have feelings for her, she's a psych major and says I have psychopathic tendencies. She says I have a deficiency in empathy and she cried one night, telling me I lack the emotions to care about anyone. But if that's true why do I care about my brother?

And why, when the single tear that dropped from the green eye, and the *Live* tattoo with the flower on the wrist of the little spitfire girl that nearly knocked herself out running into me earlier, did I hesitate?

empathy

Why did seeing her in the mirror, stunning me when I recognised her, make me not want to squeeze my fist tighter around her neck, ending the inconvenience of this cluster fuck of a job? Of all the coincidences, this one blew my mind. The aroma of her body flared the life of the man in me. She was scared and shaking, the sweat carrying her scent to me, making me human at a time I needed to be the evil I was born to be.

"You fucking coward. At least face me if you're going to kill me," she murmured.

Hell I was proud of her in that moment and that was a new feeling for me. She wasn't as weak as I first thought.

My anger grew. I didn't want to feel anything. I needed to kill her. This job had turned bad so fast. It was a shit storm that might have me tracking the client who hired me and killing him for fun. No one was supposed to be here except the parents, and it was supposed to be a quick, clean kill while they were asleep. A living girl and two dead people in a mass of blood and gore in the dining room was not how I wanted to leave the house. I had no choice. I spun her around and forced her head back into the mirror, knocking her unconscious. It shattered and splintered around her like confetti. She was beautiful; I'm cold hearted not blind. She lay there with her hair fanned out around her. She would never have felt it if I'd just ended her life, but I couldn't.

I stalked back into the shadows and waited and watched as she roused from her temporary slumber.

I will question why I stayed for my entire life.

When I broke I didn't see it. I felt it, though. The warmth left me, something inside disintegrated.

When I kill, I don't think about the person I kill, the family they might have or the person who has to find the bodies. So, to watch first hand as a girl awoke from a dream to be forced into a nightmare and see her break right in front of me was a surreal moment. It was an uncomfortable experience for me.

It's visible, a person's soul fracturing. You see their world collapse, their beliefs leave them. You see raw grief switch to anger and back again to inconsolable pain. Questions flitter through their soul. *"Why has this happened to me?"* The unanswered ache transforms their features. The shutters close over their eyes, dimming their light, shedding them of who they once were and altering them forever. The slouch of the shoulders, the drop of the mouth. Their skin turns pale. You see anger, grief and disbelief. Rage in their eyes like a storm at sea before it calms to an empty ocean. You don't just kill the mark when you do a job, you kill the spirit in the people who loved them. How will she let this change her? What will she become when she re-surfaces from the depraved actions of a soulless killer?

    She cries like a small child, calling out to her dead parents and it dislodges something inside me. I don't like seeing her shatter. I want to pick up her pieces and reassemble her, and I dislike that even more. I don't like the stained blood on her knees or the gash I created on her head. I don't like the hollow look in her eyes as she stares at the women she called Mommy. I don't like that I'm feeling. This isn't who I am. I can't be here
    I dial 911 on their house phone and leave.

I get home by seven o'clock the next morning. The house smells of sweat and sex. The blonde on our sofa is half-dressed, her make up melted from her face making her resemble a wax model too close to a flame.
    I kick the sofa, making her grumble and look up at me. Her hair is a mess and she narrows her eyes at me. "You're not Russell," she mumbles, standing up, her tits on display. They're marked with teeth marks.
    "It's Ryan, not Russell. Here," Ryan says, walking down the hall and slinging a hundred dollar bill at her.
    "What the fuck is this?" She holds up the cash. "I'm not a fucking prostitute!" She scoops her top up from the floor and pulls it over her head. It barely covers her tits. "And if I was, I'd charge more than that for the shit I let you do to me. I won't be walking right for weeks, ass-

empathy

hole." She glares at my brother.

I rub my hand over my tired eyes.

"Great, a freebie then." Ryan swipes the money from her hand. "See yourself out."

This chick doesn't even know his name then gets offended at being treated like a whore? I watch her retreat, slamming our front door behind her, the walls vibrating from the force.

A sigh leaves my body. "Leave that trash in the clubs, Ry. We've spoken about you bringing those types here. Put the video recorder away. I do not ever want to see what's on that."

I need a shower then sleep, and pray the green eyes that won't leave my mind will let me shut off.

Chapter 6

Hollow

Melody

TWO WEEKS. THAT'S ALL IT'S been but it feels like a lifetime. Police interviews make me re-tell my nightmare over and over. Being unable to bury my parents is weighing heavy on me. Apparently the police hold the bodies while they do post mortems, and sometimes they're retaken if new evidence comes to light. I have the image in my mind of my mom and dad's rotting corpses laying on a slab, waiting to be cut into and prodded. You can't control the thoughts that cloud your brain; mine are morbid, filled with flashes of the night. Hades came to taint my life, to show me true evil.

empathy

"They're letting me in the house today, Mel, so you might as well come home. No point paying out for a hotel," Markus, my half-brother, tells me. They called him when I went into shock and he's been here annoying the shit out of me ever since. He cried when they told him our father is dead. It was weird seeing a man cry, especially Markus. He's an asshole and used to argue with Dad all the time. He hated my mother and me, so to see him grieve was a surprise.

"I want to call Dad's lawyer, get things rolling," he tells me, meaning he wants his inheritance.

"I'm not ready for that, Markus. I want to bury them first."

He grabs my upper arms, squeezing the soft flesh and making me wince. "Two weeks, Mel. I'll give you two weeks then I want what's mine." His eyes are now devoid of sorrow, back to the cold blue irises that hold disfavour. Didn't take him long to be back to the heartless shit I know he is. He doesn't care that my family was murdered and I have no one left. All he cares about is money.

"You're hurting me."

He releases me with a shove and I fall back and land on the bed. Self-defence lessons will be the first thing I look up when I get back to college. I hate how nimble I am under the strength of a man's hand.

I stare up at him and shift at the uncomfortable feeling I get from the way his eyes roam over my bare legs. He had barged into my hotel room at the crack of dawn. I'm still in my nightshirt and panties, my legs exposed. He might be my brother but we have never had affection as siblings, or even friends.

"Get your shit. I need you back at the house to help sort stuff there."

A tremor rocks my body from the thought of going back. "I d... don't think I c... can go there."

"Mel, I need your help. I don't live there so I need you to show me where they kept the documents and bills. I need you to call the house cleaner and the gardener and pack their stuff up."

I can't believe what I'm hearing. "Markus, it's been two weeks. I'm not ready to pack their things up."

He rolls his eyes and kneels before me, his sweaty palms resting on my exposed thighs. He begins kneading them as he speaks. "I know this is hard, Mel. But you have to face facts. They're gone and keeping their things won't change that. We have to decide what to do with the house, and selling it with dead people's things still hanging in the wardrobe will be impossible."

Every word from his mouth is a verbal lash, whipping at my soul, ripping another layer from the frayed, dull life force keeping me tethered to this world.

I push his hands from my thighs and race past him to the bathroom. I heave into the toilet, bringing up nothing but bile that burns my throat. I feel him behind me and he sighs.

"What if I stay in the house until we decide what you want to do?"

I fold my arms over my stomach and nod. "Yeah, okay."

The thought of selling my childhood home is unbearable, even though it's now a tomb.

There's yellow tape hanging from the front door as Markus opens it and walks in but I can't move. My blood has turned to cement.

Markus turns to face me. "Come on," he says, but I'm immobile.

Tears threaten but I force them back. "I'm going back to college. I can't be here. Call me when the police release their bodies."

I turn and rush down the front steps and he follows me, gripping my wrist. "I need you here, Mel."

I shake my head. "I can't. Please let me go. I'll come back, I just need some time."

He narrows his eyes and lets go of my wrist with a shove. "Fine. Go."

I exhale and dig through my bag for my car keys. Markus had it fixed and brought back here which I'm grateful for, but I can't stay. I need distance.

Chapter 7

Forget

Melody

MY CAR EATS UP THE miles back to my dorm. It takes me less time to get back because I speed most of the way. It's just getting dark; the campus is abuzz with people coming and going, getting on with their lives like every other day. It's so crazy how one moment in time can change all future moments. What would have been? What would I be doing right now if that man hadn't taken my family?

My father's lifeless eyes flash to the forefront of my memory and acid eats my insides as the burn from the bile rising alights my throat. I can't escape the memories; they constantly replay, assaulting me with pain.

People are living their lives, never to experience death coming to steal people so important, too young, not meant to go yet. I would never wish this on any of them. Pain, anger, love, loss, confusion, grief so strong it blankets me in an icy atmosphere. How do I make it stop, make myself numb to the raging turbulence tearing my mind to shreds?

Tap, tap, tap.

I jump as knuckles hit my car window. My hand goes to my heart. I want to cry from the simple fright that would have made me laugh before. I take a deep breath and release it, opening the window. Clive's toothy grin greets me.

"Hey, sweetness. Where have you been?"

I swallow a hateful retort and shrug my shoulders. His friend is beside him, holding a bag full of booze. "So, we're heading to a party. You want to come?"

I almost laugh. Why would I go anywhere with him? But my eyes go back to the bag of 'forget fluid'. A drink, that's what I need. I've been drunk only once before, at a bonfire after senior prom. Zane held me while we slept under the stars. I'd got drunk to drown out the knowledge we would be parting, an era ending in my life.

I nod and he opens my car door. "Cool, do you want to change?"

I look down at my jean shorts and tank top. "Do I need to?"

His greedy eyes trail the length of my body, stopping on my breasts. "Not at all, but I know some girls like to wear dresses and heels to parties." I eye the bag again and he smirks. "I have plenty for you too."

Chapter 8

Need

Blake

I'VE FOLLOWED THIS LITTLE SHIt for a week, waiting for him to fuck up. I decided to go against my nature and not kill him. Instead, I'll use the law to teach him a lesson. I'm an asshole but I don't go around killing everyone I have a grievance with, even if I want to.

After Ryan's run-in with this bully, things haven't calmed down. , instead they escalated, the fucker tripped Ryan down some stairs, breaking his arm. To say the need for his blood on my hands is strong would be an understatement. My brother's not perfect but he's my brother and I'll protect him no matter what.

I follow him as he leaves his dorm with his best friend. He's carrying a bag filled with bottles of alcohol. They walk across the parking lot and stop next to a sporty BMW. He raps his knuckles on the window and talks to whoever is inside. When he opens the door, the grin on his face tells me he either just won the lottery or the person in the car is someone he's interested in. Tanned, toned legs, little jean shorts fitted over a sexy as sin ass, small waist, perfect tits, full lips.

Melody Masters.

She's Ryan's age, turned twenty last month. Only sibling is a half-brother who hired me for the job. She has an aunt on her mother's side, no living grandparents. She's completely alone now. I've obsessed over the details of the job since that night, getting all the information on the girl who has the power to stop me from being me. I should have known it was her from the number on her license plate. I've memorised every detail I can get about her. It's been two weeks since I watched her break, and two weeks of dreaming about her green eyes as a single tear leaked free. Two weeks of going over and over that night, and how I should have done things differently.

I follow them as they walk across the campus and end up at a frat house. She's not dressed in the skimpy outfits like most of the girls going in there but she still gains attention; a beacon in a dark ocean. She's unique. The fact she's even here two weeks after her parents were brutally slain is unbelievable, unless she's changed. Unless she let the winter ice freeze over the warmth and is now like me... indifferent.

Clive can't stop eye raping her as she stands looking uncomfortable, stepping from one foot to the other, her hands fidget at her side, her eyes scanning everything but him. She nudges the prick's arm and gestures towards the bag his friend is holding. He reaches for it and pulls out a bottle. They make their way around the house to the backyard where the party is in full swing. I blend in to a crowd of guys laughing and catcalling at a girl whose top is completely transparent; her tits are on full display reminding me I haven't got laid in a couple of weeks and I need a release. I stay in the background, watching as Melody accepts a red cup from a guy standing at a keg, filling drinks for everyone. She takes a shot from the dick who brought her here and shrugs off his over-familiar hand, shaking her head at him. He pouts like a woman and offers her another shot which she necks then hands the empty cup to him. We have officers who give talks about accepting open drinks from people at parties in high school. She is being flippant with her safety and it irritates me. The fact I'm getting irritated irritates me further. A growl crawls up my throat but I focus my energy and push it back down. The friend that came with them seems to be glued to a bottle while he watches them, and I bide my time on the outer edge looking in, waiting.

The night wears on with more of the same. Her goal is clearly to get wasted, and they all look pretty much there. The best friend can hardly stand, he looks like he's about to fall in the pool. I find the head brother of the fraternity and suggest he makes dick take his friend home before he has an accident and it comes down bad on the house. He thanks me for the heads up and makes his way towards Clive, throwing his keys in his direction. "Take my truck and get your buddy home. He's wasted."

"Sure, man."

I shake my head and follow them to the front of the house, take the plates and call it in. Clive forces his friend in to the truck and turns. "You coming Melody?"

I walk up behind her and place my hands on her shoulders. Her body stiffens under my touch.

"Tell him to come back for you." Her breathing accelerates.

"Come back for me," she chokes out. He narrows his eyes and taps his fingers against his leg "Why not just come with me? We can go somewhere quieter. Talk and stuff"

"And stuff" the little piss ant. "Just come back for me" she reinforces. "Don't leave this spot then" he commands before sighing, jumping in the truck and taking off.

Her body trembles under my hand.

"Hey, calm down." I turn her to face me. There are tears in her eyes and her chest is heaving from her deep breaths. Green eyes roam my face, her head tilts then she lifts her hand to slap me.

"You can't just come up behind people like that you, you ass."

My eyebrows shoot up as I hold her wrist up a few inches from my face. She's panting now, eyes searching mine before dropping to my lips, and her tongue darts out to wet her own. I drop her wrist and step back. "I was stopping you from being stupid."

Her brows furrow. "What?"

I point in the direction the truck took off in. "He was drunk driving, so unless you wanted to end up as road kill, you can thank me and stop trying to fucking hit me."

She rubs her delicate wrist where I'd gripped her. "I wasn't going to go with him, I can't stand him." Her green eyes bore into mine. "You're him, aren't you?" My heart beat stops for a brief moment. I stand mute. "The guy I bumped into a couple of weeks ago?"

I release the breath I was holding. Fuck, what is wrong with me?

"You're not weak." I speak without thinking it through. Her eyes soften and a small smile tilts her lips.

"Yeah? I feel pretty weak and I'm sorry for calling you a fuck." She chuckles then looks away, abashed. God, hearing the word *fuck* coming from those lips makes my dick stir.

"Fucking dick, I think it was." I raise an eyebrow.

She smiles and nods. "Not my finest insult. I think you knocked the sense out of me that day." She looks off into the night; she's gone somewhere in her mind. That's when I realise she's gone back to that day, that night her world changed.

I checked and re-checked the details on that hit. If her brother wasn't the only family she had left, I would have killed him for the mess.

"Hey." I reach out and stroke her arm. Her olive skin feels like silk under my fingers. "I'm sorry."

She shakes her head, mistaking my gesture as affection when I just wanted to pull her back from her memories so I didn't have to feel the aggression and unsettled pandemonium rattling around in my mind when I think of her and why she still has a pulse.

"So, is this your house?" she asks.

I smirk. She thinks I belong to a frat house. How wrong she is. I shake my head. "No I don't go here."

"Then why are you here?"

I look around, taking in the overflowing party goers, the loud annoying music that is just a beat and an out of tune bitch hollering into a mic. "I was looking for someone."

She fidgets, kicking at imaginary dirt. I take in the length of her bare legs. She's stunning but seems insecure. How can she not know how attractive she is?

"Oh, okay. Well I'll let you go find them." She smiles but it doesn't reach her eyes.

"They already left." I slip my hands into my jeans pockets and look down at her. "Do you want me to walk you home?"

She nods. She's a little unsteady on her feet from the alcohol she's consumed.

I walk beside her and have to stop her when she starts to walk into the road. My hands are on her waist, the heat from her skin seeps into my palm. Turning slowly so she's facing me, her head tilts up, her eyes half lidded. She reaches up onto her tiptoes and crushes her soft, full lips against mine. She tastes sweet, like cherries and a hint of vodka. My arms fasten around her waist, pulling her supple body into mine. My lips taste hers; her tongue shoots out and into my parted mouth. My head wages war with my cock but I wouldn't be who I am if I let weak impulses control me.

I push her back. "What are you doing?"

I need time to clear the clouded thoughts raging in my head. She makes me *feel!* She made my heart speed up and my skin vibrate with electricity when she kissed me. I can't have that. Why the fuck does she have an effect on me?

"I just want to forget for a little while," she whispers, stroking her hands up my arms and into my hair. She reaches up onto her tiptoes again but I step away.

"You're acting irresponsibly. I could be anyone and you let me walk you home, and then you throw yourself at me. Do you want to be murdered? Raped? Then again, you can't rape the willing, so maybe you want to be used as a slut for a night?"

I'm being harsh, but I *am* harsh. I need to remember who I am. I need her to not want or like me.

She drops her hands and steps away from me. Torment swirls in those hypnotic eyes of hers and then I see pity. Understanding changes her features like she's just solved a puzzle.

"Wow, you really are a fucking dick. A bitter fucking dick. If I was male and just wanted a bit of comfort, a kiss to help rid myself of memories that plague me it would be okay, but because I'm a girl, that makes me a slut who wants to be raped and murdered? I didn't ask you to have sex with me, I just kissed you." She runs her hands through her long, dark waves. "Thanks for stopping me. I went further than I meant to, but hell, there isn't enough soap that would get your bitterness off me if I went any further. I clearly am a poor judge of character."

She turns and heads back towards the dorms, alone in the dark, her words echoing around my brain. She is so feisty I can't decide if I want to squeeze her throat and watch her eyes gloss over with tears, or rip her tiny shorts off and bury my dick inside her, making her scream, making her so fucking dirty she'll never get clean. I stay back but follow her to make sure she makes it home. I didn't kill her when she came home unexpectedly that night, so I refuse to let anyone else do it. I know what lurks in the shadows. I won't let anything bad happen to her that's not my doing.

God, I really am a fucking dick.

When I see her light turn on in her room I pull out my cell and text Abby.

You busy?

It takes her less than thirty seconds to reply.

Yes, I'm at a party, why?

She knows why. I only ever message her when I want to fuck.

You know why.

Well, you'll have to find some other idiot

empathy

to be your hole for the night. I'm here with a guy.

That's new. My hole for the night? Guess she really is fed up with my coldness towards her. Shame, she has a lethal mouth. I don't bother replying.

I head back towards the party where I know I'll be able to take my pick from all the half-dressed sluts there. I just need to get laid so I can stop thinking about her, stop myself from feeling shit I don't need to be feeling.

I spot Abby when I reach the party. Small world. She's dancing with her girlfriends, not one guy anywhere near her.

You can't make me jealous Abby, so don't play a game you can't win.

I scan the crowd and notice Abby's best friend by the bar with Abby's phone.

I smile. The devious little bitch, pretending to be Abby. I walk up behind her and look over her shoulder as she texts a reply to me.

"What the fuck's your problem?" I ask, making her jump.

She turns and twists up her face in disgust. "You are. She drops us as soon as you call and you treat her like shit. She deserves better."

I grab her hand and drag her outside, around to the side of the house. She doesn't try to break my grasp; she fumbles along in her stupid shoes that she can't walk in, clanking across the wooden decking. "What are you doing?"

"Showing you why she drops you as soon as I call."

I push her against the wall, reaching for the hem of her dress and yanking it up to her waist. She gasps but doesn't stop me. Her chest is brushing against mine as it rises and falls from her ragged breaths. I bring my lips to her neck and trace a line up to her earlobe, biting gently. Her perfume makes my nose sting and my tongue taste disgusting. This chick needs to lay off the cheap fragrance she's laced her body in.

"What are you doing? Blake, stop it, you're with Abby."

Her ragged pants tell me she'll let me do whatever the fuck I want.

"Abby knows what she has with me. Sex, that's all I can give her and all I want. She knows this."

I slip my hand to the front of her panties, and she gasps and grabs my hand. She's dripping wet. "No, stop. I can't. Abby loves you."

I pull back so I can look into her lust-filled brown eyes. "Then you're a shitty friend, sabotaging her by texting me. Now, instead of her getting to be with me, I'll be fucking some slut tonight."

Her hands rears back but I grab her wrist and laugh. What is it with women trying to slap me?

"I'm not a slut," she spits.

I look down at her exposed panties and smirk. "I didn't mean you, but if the shoe fits. And I stand firm on the shitty friend statement. Look at you, out here with the guy your friend's in love with." I tut at her and shake my head.

Anger then guilt fills her eyes and her head drops. I test her further by slipping my hand back in her panties. Her face lifts, her teeth biting into her lip, confliction raging in her gaze. Her hand slips over the top of mine and pushes me further until I'm almost at her entrance. She's soaking wet and ready for me to do whatever I want, but I already have. I grin at her and pull my hand out swiping her juices across her lips. Her nose scrunches. I step back, her hands reach out for me, making me chuckle, a dark laugh at how pathetic she is. I walk back through the house passing Abby as I go, not acknowledging her. I've been a complete asshole and I don't feel bad. I don't feel anything for them which is normal, but she, *Green Eyes,* is still niggling away at me.

Chapter 9

Patience

Ryan

I WALK UP THE STAIRS and take my seat in creative writing, waiting for Sean to make his appearance. He's the guy I got partnered with when Melody didn't show for the assignment. She's been AWOL for over two weeks and hasn't replied to any of my texts. I wonder if she dropped out.

"Hey, man," Sean says as he sits next to me in Melody's seat. I tilt my head in acknowledgment. "You want to hit a bar with me tonight?"

I look over at him. His wavy blond hair sits neatly against his forehead and his pale green eyes have a look of innocence. I know he's gay, even if he tries hard not to show it. I caught him checking me out when I had him over to work on our project.

"Will there be willing women at this bar?" I ask and he flinches slightly.

"Isn't there always? We are in college," he replies, his voice losing enthusiasm.

The door swings open and Melody saunters in. Her brown hair shields her face from view but her presence is unmistakable. She walks over to our T.A who has been running this class. He smiles softly at her while speaking in a hushed tone and places a hand on her shoulder in a comforting gesture. She nods and turns towards the stairs. Tucking her hair behind her ear she looks up at me. There's something different about her. She's lost weight and her eyes hold… grief. She makes her way up the stairs, her jean skirt giving me a wonderful view of her toned legs. Reaching my seat she looks at Sean who doesn't hesitate to shift over, leaving the seat next to me empty for her.

"Thank you," she says, and slides into the seat he vacated. "I'm so sorry I missed our assignment arrangement."

"I texted you."

"My phone got misplaced. I haven't caught up with messages and things yet." I search her eyes for the truth and that's what I see. Truth and sorrow. "I've had a really shitty couple of weeks, Ryan. I could use a friend right now so can you just accept that I wouldn't deliberately ignore you and let me make it up to you?"

I raise an eyebrow. "Make it up to me how?"

I half smile and she relaxes. "Get your mind out of the gutter. I'll buy you lunch and drinks if you agree to come out with me to get trashed tonight."

"Find a way to reply to me in future." I narrow my eyes at her, watching her shocked expression for a second before I relax my features. "My mind likes the gutter, and you're on. Sean and I were just talking about hitting a club tonight."

She turns to Sean. "Do you mind me tagging along?"

He studies her for a few minutes then looks at me. "Of course not. The more the merrier."

She turns and nods at me. "Thank you."

I want to ask her why her week was so bad but I don't. We all like

empathy

to keep secrets and have dark corners in our minds that don't need anyone shining light on. I can see her eyes have darkened; maybe hers are even darker than mine. She's troubled, haunted and I want to delve into her darkness and swim in her hurt, but I'll wait.

The rest of the class passes quickly, Melody never once touching pen to paper. "Where are we going for lunch?" I ask as we leave the class.
"Melody!" Clive calls out her name and she turns. "What happened to you last night? I went back for you."
She shrugs. "I went home. I got tired."
His narrowed eyes in my direction cause a curve in my lip, my smile taunting him. Taking her wrist he gently coaxes her away from me but she pulls free.
"Listen, Clive. I thought I made myself clear last night when your hands groped my ass and I told you I'm not interested."
He glares at her. "Then why did you come to the party with me?"
"Because it was a party and I wanted to have fun. Just because I went to a party with you two," she gestures to Clive and his wannabe boyfriend, "doesn't mean it was an invitation to grope me."
She turns and leaves him heaving with anger. I follow her and sling my arm over her shoulder, just to wind him up further. She notices the cast peeking out of my shirt and wrapping around my thumb. "Shit. What happened?"
I smirk and point behind her. "He happened. He tripped me on some stairs."
She turns to glare at the shrinking figure of Clive. "That son of a bitch!" Sean has fallen in step next to me and he chuckles.
"So, just so we're clear on this, just because you're coming out with us that doesn't mean we can freely grope your ass?" I ask with a straight face, earning a slap to my chest and a giggle. It's a pretty sound but a thunder storm rolls into her eyes, making her laugh falter and stop abruptly. She is probably the only female I've ever been around for longer than five minutes and not got bored of. I don't like the company of women... or men really. It's hard to find someone on my intellectual level. People enrage me but there are a rare few who intrigue.

She looks between Sean and me and lifts a shoulder. "Depends how many drinks you buy me."

We both laugh, only mine is for show. "Didn't you agree you're buying the drinks?"

She smiles. "Does that mean I get to grope your asses?"

Sean pushes the door to the exit and gives her a wink. "Hey I'm cheap. If you're buying, grope away. Oh, and I heard Clive got arrested last night for drunk driving."

I look at Sean. "How is he out so fast?"

He shrugs. "His dad is a lawyer, a good one." Of course he is. "Frankie's diner?" Sean asks as we exit the building. I look at Melody and she nods.

"Sure," I say. I don't care where I eat. I eat to fuel my body, not for the pleasure of the taste.

We slide into a booth and order burgers, fries and shakes.

"So how was your trip? You went home, right?" I ask.

Melody's eyes shine like polished glass, the color drains from her face and she fidgets, twisting her hands together. Her eyes flick to the front door as the bell chimes, her breathing increases. *Panic attack.* I turn and watch a couple of officers enter. I know them as Ryes and Mills, they're friends of Blake. I nod my head towards them. They walk to our table and I look back at Melody. Her eyes are trained on them as they come closer, her head subtly shakes. I reach out for her as a hand lands on my shoulder.

"Hey, Ry. How's school?" Ryes asks. Melody shifts in her seat and her breathing becomes more controlled.

"Usual."

He looks at my hand grasping Melody's and grins. "We're having a barbeque a week on Saturday. Your brother will be there. You should come. Bring your girl."

"Excuse me, I need the bathroom," Sean murmurs.

I scoot out to let him pass and watch as he walks to the bathroom running his hands through his hair. Melody follows my eyes and smiles.

"We'll see," I reply.

The waitress appears, setting our drinks down.

empathy

"Well, good to see you. Stay out of trouble." Ryes laughs, pats my shoulder and leaves us.

"You okay?" I ask Melody.

She smiles nervously. "How do you know police officers?"

"My brother is one."

She nods but she's gone somewhere in her mind. I want to pry. I want to be in there seeing what she's seeing, thinking. I want to question her but I don't. I live in my head a lot and hate people knocking at the door I never want to open in front of witnesses.

"Hey, can I get in?" Sean asks, coming back to the table.

Ha! Good timing. I move over and let him slide in.

Chapter 10

Wasted

Melody

WHEN RYAN ASKED IF I went home, flashes of my parents filled my mind. Then the police officers entered the diner, my mind connected the two and I thought I was going to pass out. Darkness closed in around me as they came closer. Ryan's hands grounded me. I was grateful he didn't pry into my total freak out. Everything reminds me of them, waking up and not receiving my dad's daily inspirational texts. Something as simple as pulling my clothes on reminds me of the shopping trip Mom took me on to buy them. Making breakfast reminds me I will never taste her home cooking again. My car reminds me of Dad. The smell of the warm air as the sun graces the surface, heating the concrete, reminds me of summer vacations. I can't escape them and I need to because with every good memory of them comes the memory of their ugly deaths, their pain, their fear. My pain, my fear. I can't believe their killer touched me. The hands that stole the lives of the only two people I loved held my life in his palm and didn't take it. Unless he did, and this is what hell is.

I swipe the stray tear that leaks down my cheek. I need to numb it out. My phone chimes to alert me to missed calls and texts from Markus. I can't believe he uploaded his number before finally giving me back my phone.

```
"I need you here."
"You're being a brat."
"I need the codes to the safe."
"The lawyers won't speak to me. They say
Dad's lawyer is on vacation"
```

He makes me want to scream and tear at his flesh until he feels some kind of pain. How can he be so cold and selfish?

I throw my phone on the desk. My dorm room offers no comfort. My dad paid for me to have my own room so I would be alone, and God, I really am alone. Empty space like my ever-growing empty life. I haven't made any friends except for Ryan, and my friends at home have all flown the nest and are out living their lives. I haven't even heard from Zane. *Home.* I guess it isn't home anymore, it's a crime scene. A grave, a nightmare that has imprinted itself onto every memory I have of that house.

The guy from the party, the one who knocked me on my ass that day, is the one thing I grab onto. When my thoughts stray, I think of him and how shocked I was at how rude someone could be. I memorized every detail so I can focus only on bumping into him that day. His earthy scent, the baritone of his voice, the structure of his stance; that's how I knew it was him at the party, and then he turned out to be an even bigger asshole then I first thought. I can't believe I lost my inhibitions and kissed him. He's beautiful up close but his eyes are guarded. Urgh! Why does he have to be a contradiction?

I grab my wash kit to take a shower. I let the tears fall, hoping they will take the emptiness with them. I feel so lost, willing myself to melt into the water and let it carry me away as it runs down the drain and out to sea. Lonely is more than a feeling, it's a manifestation weighing heavily on my heart, a burden crushing, suffocating me, consuming my thoughts. *You're all alone, you have no one. You are no one's.* It's on my skin, coating me in a cold, clammy mist, taking my warmth. Why would someone do this? Why them? Why me? Why? I need to shut my brain off.

I towel myself dry and slip into skinny jeans, a black tank top and biker boots. I dry and straighten my hair, leaving my face free of makeup. My feet carry me in a haze to the bar, my mind functioning on auto pilot, commanding myself to stop thinking, to just exist.

By the time Ryan and Sean arrive I'm drinking my fourth shot. I wave them over to the bar and signal for the bartender to refill.

"Hey, you started without us?" Sean asks.

I grin, the warmth of the alcohol taking the chill from my haunted spirit.

"Yep, so you better catch up." I slap the bar and throw another shot back. The bartender raises an eyebrow and cocks his head to Ryan.

"Yeah, fill her up," Ryan tells him.

I scowl at the bartender; he's cute with messy blond hair, defined arms, and blue eyes. "I don't need permission," I warn him with a glare and hand my credit card to him. "Keep them coming."

He smiles and takes my card, wrapping his hand over mine, keeping my attention on him. "I was just looking out for you, sweetheart. You've had quite a few, you'll be numb soon if you keep this up."

I pull my hand back. "That's the plan."

The humid air sticks to me, thick with sweat and the essence of sexual tension and alcohol. The thumping baseline from the DJ, Sean and Ryan's hands encompassing my hips, one in front one behind, veils out all other thoughts. I'm floating on a cloud of intoxication.

"Let's go back to my place," Ryan shouts in my ear.

He grabs my hand, and my feet follow as he pulls me through the club. The fresh air hits my face and fills my lungs. My head swims, my vision blurs, and my legs feel like they are made of jello. A giggle erupts from my chest and then turns into chest-shaking sobs. "Hey, shh. What's wrong?" I know its Ryan cooing in my ear and I let the comfort of his closeness engulf me. My eyelids flutter closed.

The little men inside my head trying to hammer their way out make me groan and stir. My mouth is so dry I have to peel my lips apart. Last night rushes into my mind, then the reason I wanted to get wasted pushes through. *Mom, Dad, gone. Murdered.*

I feel shattered, particles separate from my true being. Now I'm just dust on the wind, ash on a burned out flame. The hand that wrapped around my throat in that house is still there, squeezing tight, robbing me of my soul.

I pull the blankets back and look around the unfamiliar room. It's neat, almost too neat. My eyes sting from the crude exposure to the sun beaming through the open blinds. I slip my legs free from the bed and wince as my feet make contact with the cold wooden floor. Tiptoeing to the door I sigh with relief when the bathroom door is open just a couple feet from this room. I come face to face with a mirror as I enter, sending a shiver through my veins. My hands tremble; it's the same whenever I look in a mirror since that night.

"It's okay, Mel. You're okay," I reassure myself, and look back up into the mirror. I don't recognise the distorted image looking back at me. My dark hair lacks its usual shine, my eyes are unfocused. God, I drank too much. I look down at the panties and tank top I'm wearing, a groan leaving my lips.

A shadow passes behind me and I freeze. It morphs into the form of a guy. Fear steals my breath, and my heart slows then picks up speed, beating erratically. A hand on my shoulder makes the contents of last night's drinking rush out of me in a burning torrent. The sting in my throat makes my eyes water. The retching sends an ache through my ribs.

"Fuck, why does he bring women home with him?" the male

grumbles behind me.

    I spit, unladylike, into the sink and turn the tap to wash away the bile. I look up and stare. *No way*. His eyes are the color of gun metal fused with dark green flecks. His dark hair is swept back off his face. His white shirt is pulled from his slacks, a few buttons undone. My eyes seek out the strong muscle of his chest on display. I flick my eyes back to his and watch him as he gazes back at me.

Chapter 11

Déjà vu

Blake

NO FUCKING WAY. I'M LOOKING into the green eyes that keep me up at night. She's standing in MY bathroom in her underwear. Fuck, she's in her underwear. My eyes drag themselves down her body. Tight and tanned, she looks so smooth I want to reach out and touch her skin. Her round tits fill out the tank she's wearing, and my appraisal is having an effect on her, tightening her nipples into hard little pebbles. Saliva fills my mouth. Her legs shift, drawing my eyes to that perfect v between her thighs, her black lace panty shorts giving me a hip jerk reaction. Fuck, she's smooth down there; I can see the folds through the lace. My dick stirs and hardens. What the fuck is she doing in here?

"Oh, hey. She's with me," Ryan says, walking up behind me and patting me on the back. He skims by and grabs her hand, leading her past me. It's a reaction I've never had before, an urge driven by emotions I've never possessed. I grab her wrist, halting their steps. Her green orbs bore into mine and her lips part. *Fuck, fuck, fuck.* She came here and stayed the night with Ry. Ry's sexual preference is not for young, green-eyed girls like her. She came here and fucked Ry? Why does that twist my gut?

"What are you doing, Blake? Let go of her."

I clear the confusion clogging my head. Releasing her wrist, the one with her LIVE tattoo and flower, I raise my eyes to meet my brother's. He's studying me, searching for answers I don't want to give him.

"I've told you about bringing your whores here, Ry."

Her gasp draws my eyes to hers. "Screw you," she breathes and rushes from the bathroom.

Ry pushes my chest. I look down at the place his hand just left, then back up to him with a cocked brow. He has never cared enough to have a reaction before.

"Don't. She's not like them, she's different and I don't need you scaring her. I can do that on my own if I want to." He turns and leaves me speechless.

I love my brother, he can be irresponsible when it comes to bringing club trash home, but I've never wanted to hurt him before now, before her. The thought of him being in there with her. *She's different.*

Fuck my life! This girl has messed up my head. I faltered at that house and didn't kill her. I watched her break and now she haunts me when I try to sleep. She occupies my thoughts when I'm awake and is now in my house, in my brother's bed. Who is she and why was she sent to cause bedlam to my mind?

I finish getting ready and make my way downstairs. I must have missed them coming out of his room because now they're in the kitchen, drinking coffee. They're both dressed. Her eyes bore into me as I make my way to the pot and fill my cup. I'm about to take a gulp when some blond guy comes down the stairs in a pair of boxers. What the actual fuck? He blushes like a woman when he sees me.

"Hi." He head nods to me and then looks at Melody who is sup-

empathy

pressing a grin

"Did I miss a party?" I ask, cocking my brow as Ry smirks.

"You couldn't handle my kinda parties, brother."

Melody's eyes widen. "Ry, thank you for taking care of me, and you too, Sean but I'm never drinking again." She puts her cup in the sink, her arm brushing mine. Even a subtle touch makes my dick come to life. "I need to head back to my dorm." She waves over her shoulder on her way out of my house. That was a real casual goodbye.

"She's not your usual type," I say, then look to the practically naked blond guy standing there like a statue. "Go get dressed, party's over."

Ryan's eyes follow the retreating guy while answering with no emotion in his tone. "They're just some people from college. The guy you just gave a stroke is Sean, and the female you insulted in the bathroom is Melody. Although she fascinates me I'm not fucking her."

Why does that make my body relax? Okay, not going to dwell on that. I leave before he can read anything into the small smile that tilts my lips. Like I figured, a girl like her wouldn't be into bed hopping with a kinky bastard, even if she did try it on with me. I head to work without another word.

Chapter 12

Boundaries

Ryan

I FELT A LITTLE TIRED as I sat sipping my coffee. I didn't really like drinking alcohol but with Melody practically tipping shots into my mouth last night it couldn't be avoided. My mind replays everything that happened over in my mind.

Carrying Melody to the cab; she was troubled, even in her alcohol-induced sleep. So, alcohol was going to be how she coped with things. The turbulence in her eyes told me she was battling to cope. I wanted to ask her, get her to open up to me but even with her drunken tongue, she didn't say anything about her trip home. The reason she

empathy

was gone for so long and the reason behind her sorrow remained a secret.

Sean climbed in next to me and kept glancing at Melody, asleep, wrapped in my embrace. I gave the cab driver my address and we rode in silence for the ten minute journey. When we pulled up, Sean was hesitant, clearly not sure if he was welcome to come in. I was curious if he would let me take an unconscious Melody into my house without saying anything. He'd only known me for two weeks.

The cab driver broke the stare between Sean and me. "Is she okay? Do you know her?"

I smiled. "She's our best friend, had a rough break up. Sean, baby, get the door." The cab driver scrunched his nose, looked between me and Sean then nodded. Sean was stunned, staring at me.

I kicked his ankle. "Door."

He opened his door and rushed round to get mine. I pulled myself out of the cab, not easy with another person attached to you. "Pay the driver."

Sean scrabbled for his wallet, giving the driver a twenty and tapping the roof of the car. The driver took off, kicking up gravel as he departed.

"My key's in my front pocket."

Sean's eyes bulged then he slipped his hand in my pocket, his pale skin displaying a blush as it painted his entire face. He couldn't make eye contact and I suppressed a laugh. He was so transparent and he didn't even know it. Pathetic. He unlocked the door and followed me in. I went straight upstairs and placed Melody on my bed. "Take her pants and shoes off. I need to piss." Sean squirmed a little, looking between us. "Sean."

"Why did you tell the cab driver she's our best friend?"

I narrowed my eyes. "He was asking questions, because two college guys coming home with a passed out chick looks a bit suspect, no? At least if he thought we were more interested in fucking each other than her, he'd shut up."

The crimson from earlier reappeared. I stepped closer to him, leaning down so I was right in his face. I bit my lip and watched his eyes zone in on the action. "He doesn't need to know how much we love pussy, and how much we want to taste Melody under our tongues."

He flinched and stepped away from me. "She's out of it, Ry."

Yeah, that's the reason he doesn't want to taste her. God, if there was a time for him to just tell me he bats for other team this would have been it.

I turned my back on him and called over my shoulder. "I like my women to know what's happening to them, Sean. God, what do you think I am?" I grinned, knowing he was wringing his hands together with anxiety.

Once I did my business, I showered, leaving the door open so Sean could see me in the mirror, reflecting my wet image down the hallway where he stood, fighting the urge to stroke his hard dick. I turned the taps off and stepped out, letting him see me in the flesh. His breathing increased, his eyelids at half-mast. I gave him a full minute to soak me in. I maintain a good physique. I have a smaller frame than Blake; where he's broad and built, I'm trim and lean. I have a six pack that takes two hundred sit ups a day to maintain.

"Sean, what the fuck are you doing?"

His eyes snapped up to mine, widening when he realised he'd been staring at my junk, and his jeans proved what he'd tried to hide.

He turned, walking into the wall before stumbling around and rushing into my room mumbling, "I needed to use the bathroom."

I strode into my room behind him, still buck naked, grabbing a towel from my stash that I like to keep just for my use. I dried off and grabbed a pair of boxers. I noticed Sean did as I asked and made Melody more comfortable.

Jumping into the bed next to her, smelling the hint of apples embedded on her skin, I sighed. Sweet, sweet Melody. How easy you would be to take.

"Sean, go use the bathroom then make yourself comfy on the futon, man. I need to sleep."

He nodded.

I pretended to sleep when he came back but I lay awake for most of the night.

I woke to the sun assaulting my eyes. Fuck, I forgot to close the blinds. I noticed Melody wasn't in bed. Sean was still asleep on the futon. I heard voices so I followed them and found Blake in the bath-

empathy

room talking to Melody. She looked worse for wear but still attractive.

After Blake acting out of character around her, I surmised he'd met her before but where? And why, when he thought I hadn't touched her, did he smile?

I look at the clock knowing if I have another coffee I will be late for class where I plan to plant the little treat I worked on last night for Jacob and Clive. Flicking on the switch to make a fresh pot, I sit and let my mind unfold theories.

Chapter 13

Friends

Melody

WHEN I LEAVE RYAN'S HOUSE, I realise I don't have my car with me. I restrain the groan and begin the long walk home.

The walk is refreshing. The reckless behaviour of the night before has left an impression on my skull, and I need to breathe fresh air and walk off the dull thud. I'm just grateful Ryan and Sean turned out to be trustworthy, although Ryan can't make coffee to save his life. The cup he made me has left a tar layer on my tongue, not helping the queasy stir in my stomach.

My mind wanders to Blake. Ha! So, the arrogant ass has a name and he's Ryan's brother which means he is the police officer. How can someone paid to protect and serve be such an asshole, not even helping to pick up someone he knocked over? And the blow off he gave me about me kissing him, and then staring at me with such intensity in his bathroom. The air could have ignited if our bodies struck each other.

Ryan quizzed me about how I knew him when he dragged me back to his room, and I was truthful. I don't know him. I didn't even know his name until Ryan enlightened me. Blake. It suits him; a strong, confident name to match the aura of superiority he gives off.

The toot from an approaching car startles me and I nearly slip into the ditch I've been avoiding the entire trek home. A window lowers and a bright red-haired head pops out.

"Hey," the bright cheery voice from the girl who smiled whenever she saw me chirps. We have journalism class together and she seems to want to interact with me but I've yet to introduce myself.

I tilt my head to look in the car; her sister is driving. They have the same fire red hair and almost black eyes which give them an intense, almost supernatural look.

"Cherry and Red." She grins, flicking her finger to her and her sister. My eyebrow raises. "Nicknames, clearly." She giggles.

"Argh, there's a car coming up behind me, Cherry," Red screeches. Cherry rolls her eyes and sticks her arm out of the car, waving for the other car to pass, and receives a horn blast from the driver as he overtakes.

"Need a ride?"

I nod and they pull to a stop for me to leap in. I barely get the door closed before Red pulls out and guns the engine.

"Thanks."

I receive two smiles in the review mirror. Cherry has a dimple, her features slightly younger than her sister's. "So, we see you around campus and we share a class. We also saw you last night with Ryan and Sean."

It isn't a question, it's an observation. They must have been at the same club last night, which isn't a surprise since it's popular with students.

"Yeah," is all I offer. They share a look.

Red taps her fingers on the steering wheel. "So, you came from

Ryan's house?"

"Yeah, I stayed over."

Both sets of onyx eyes grow large and Cherry turns in her seat to face me.

"Oh my God! What was he like? Red stocked her pantie drawer with her slut attire when she first laid eyes on Ryan in the hopes of giving him a kink fest and pubic floss."

My mouth drops and a giggle erupts from me. "Pubic floss?"

Red glares at her sister.

"Yeah, you know, getting pubic hair stuck in his teeth from..." Cherry winks, pointing to her sister's lap and gaining her a slapped hand.

"You may be a sascrotch, Cherry. I have mine waxed!"

"Sascrotch?" I hold my stomach from the laughter.

"She's like a wild bush down there!" Red smirks. "So..." she continues, expectant for me to spill the sexploits of Ryan.

"I'm sorry to disappoint but he was the perfect gentlemen, and Sean was there too. We just crashed."

Their faces drop, and Cherry spins in her seat to face forward. "Hmm Sean, would have been awesome spit roast by those two."

Her sister's eyes narrow before all three of us burst into laughter.

Pulling up at the dorm, I'm apprehensive to get out of the car. The fifteen minutes I've been in here, I haven't even thought about my parents. Guilt swarms me. How can I laugh when they are cold on a slab right now?

"Melody?"

I shake my head to focus on them. "Sorry, what?"

Cherry's smile is really pretty, lighting up her whole face. "Red and I are going shopping tomorrow. You want to come?"

I could use a few things and spending time out of my dorm would be nice. "Sure." I return her smile.

"Great, we can go straight from class. Meet us in the quad."

I reach for the door handle, offering thanks for the ride. My insides trip when I notice the suits standing near a black unmarked car. Their eyes find me and hold me. I make my way towards my dorm but stop when they approach me. "Miss Masters? Melody Masters?" The tall one with salt and pepper hair asks.

empathy

His friend removes his glasses; blue eyes shine at me with sympathy. I nod to confirm I'm me.

"I'm Detective Roberts, and this is Detective Donovan." They both flash their badges. "We need to have a word, if that's okay?"

Leading them to my dorm, I ignore the stares from my peers. "Come in," I murmur, gesturing to my room. They both enter, closing the door behind them. My hands are shaking and I can't stop them so I fold my arms across my chest, hugging myself.

"We have been made aware of your situation, Miss Masters." My eyes look everywhere but at them. "We're sorry for your loss." Ha! No they're not. They don't know the value of who was taken from me; the words that spill from his mouth are scripted.

"Why are you here?" I ask.

The older guy clears his throat, looking at the younger one. *Passing the buck*. The younger one steps forward, his voice gentle like he's speaking to a child. "Melody, we have reason to believe you may not be safe."

My breath hitches. "He let me go."

Donavan's eyes study my face before he reaches forward, touching his hand to my elbow, guiding me backwards until my knees collide with my bed. "Take a seat."

My body complies, lowering to sit.

He kneels so he's at eye level with me. "Melody, with the way in which your parents were murdered, we can't understand why the perp would leave you unharmed."

I scoff. "Oh, he left his mark, Detective."

He flinched from my brazen bravery. "I'm sorry, that's not what I meant. We believe he may not be done with you."

Closing my eyes, I try to let what he's saying soak in. "Have you got any leads on who did this?"

He stands. "The investigation is ongoing at this moment. I'm sorry we don't have anything to bring you some peace, but criminals this reckless, they always mess up somewhere and we will find him when he does." My heart hurts. I meet his eyes and see determination shining back at me. "We want you to come to the station and answer a few questions for us. We also want to keep a tail on you for a while."

I shudder, my hands stroking down my arms, the cold chill blowing from the inside. "What does that mean?"

Salt and pepper guy steps forward. "Don't worry, Miss Masters. We will just have a detective keeping an eye on your dorm to look for anyone acting suspicious."

My eyes grow big.

"It's just protocol, Melody. When we believe a victim to be in further danger, we want to be cautious and take precautions to be on the safe side," Donavan cuts in, reaching into his pocket and pulling out a card. "You ever have questions or you remember anything, don't hesitate to call me, okay? We can bring you to the station now if you have the time?"

Slipping the card from his fingers and getting to my feet, I shake my head no "I will come down tomorrow if that's ok?". His hand rests on my shoulder. "You're not alone, Melody. We will do everything we can to bring this animal to justice."

"Donovan!" the other guy barks, gesturing with his head in the direction of the exit. His hand leaves me, and the door closes behind them as they leave.

I sink to the floor and let the tears claim me. Questions rage in my head but they lead nowhere. God, who is this guy and why didn't he just kill me?

The clock by my bed informs me I'm late for class. I can't face it now, anyway. I don't know why I'm still here, going through my routine like everything is normal, like my insides are not corroded with misery. I need to focus on the anger, the anger towards Hades, the bastard who stole my life. He has to be the devil himself. Who else could be this cruel?

Chapter 14

Murder

Blake

"A FINE?" I MOCK.

"Let it go, Braxton." Swallowing the growl at him using my last name, I leave the chief's office.

"Yo, Blake," Donovan calls to me, coming over to meet me at my desk. I tilt my head in acknowledgment. "I need a list of security guards at your brother's college, and their shifts. I figured you may already have this information as you're so protective of him."

My eyes assess him. "What's this about?"

He drops a folder on my desk. "A victim who found her parents murdered goes there, which puts her on our watch list. We have reason to believe she may still be in danger."

I kept my features relaxed as I picked up the case file, flipping through the details. "Why do you think that?"

Taking a seat, his ass parks on the edge of the desk, making it creak. "The way her folks were killed is gruesome. He enjoyed the kill. The profilers believe he's psychopathic, and if so, he shouldn't have hesitated to kill her. They think this may have been orchestrated because of her." I drop the folder and wait for him to continue. "We think he may be watching her, and might strike again. We have her brother under watch but according to her interviews, she isn't close with him and she doesn't have any other family she's close to. It was just her parents, so we don't know if, when or who he will strike again."

I fold my arms, leaning back to look up at him. "You think he's separating her from loved ones?" I want to laugh. These are detectives, profilers, and this is what they come up with.

"We think she's what drove him to commit these crimes. We have no person of interest to back it up, though."

I tap the folder. "What about the brother?"

He shakes his head. "Nope, he has an alibi and no motive." *No motive? No motive they are aware of.* "We're just waiting for the Masters' lawyer to come back from the Bahamas to question him about their financial situation, but as far as we know they're clean and this is connected to Melody."

My arms unfold and rest on my knees, my eyebrow cocking. "Melody?" I question at him using her first name.

He straightens. "Miss Masters," he corrects, his eyes gazing at the folder. "She's twenty years old and has no family. She reminds me of Emily." Emily is his wife. She lost her brother and folks in a house fire and couldn't take the grief. She tried to kill herself before she met him, and he gave her something to live for.

"I know her," I spoke out, shocking him. His head turns to me so fast it looks it could sprain.

"What?"

"She's a friend of Ryan's. She stayed overnight last night. I woke up to find her in my bathroom."

His jaw tics, eyes narrowed on me. "He taking advantage of dam-

empathy

aged women now?"

Heat soars up my spine, my body turning rigid. "Fucking watch it when you talk about my brother, Donovan. That's your only warning." Ryan has a reputation around here for bedding everyone in high school, including a lot of sisters of people we grew up around. Unfortunately, some I now work with. "They are just friends, they weren't alone."

"You think he would mind answering a few questions about her?"

I don't like this shit at all, this is the reason I don't take jobs where I live. This is my own fault. I should have been more thorough when researching the target but I focused on the brother and his background rather than delving into the fact he has a half-sister away at college. "I will talk to him and find out anything of interest."

He pats my shoulder. "Okay, good. I need you to tail her for me."

I've been watching her anyway. I can't get her out my head, so better to be doing it as the law than as a fucking stalker. "Yeah, sure."

I don't really have a choice. I'm new; young for a detective. I need to work up the ranks and that means doing the crappy jobs we would usually put a uniform officer on. They must be worried about her to use resources like this.

I need coffee. I jump up to go to the coffee pot, stopping when two women stand in my path. "Can you help her?"

I scan the sheepish girl averting her eyes, her hair lank around her face, her clothes hanging from her frail frame. "With what?" Patience is a virtue, and something I don't have much of when it comes to other human beings.

"She saw something bad but she's scared to report it."

My eyes fall back on the fidgeting girl. "What did you see?"

She shakes her head and her friend speaks for her again. "Like I said, she's scared to tell. You guys can protect her right?"

Pushing back the urge to roll my eyes and shake the jumpy bitch, I try the gentle approach; that seems to work for Donavan and the other detectives. "Listen, I can help you, protect you, but you have to give me something because right now you're being vague."

The friend scuttles forward, coming too close for my liking, her cigarette breath brushes against my chest and her eyes grow wide with excitement. "Murder." She raises her eyebrows, impressed by the fact she has information on a murder. Any normal person would be scared or saddened even, but no, she's caught up in the drama of it. Shit, we're a flawed race.

I place my hand on her shoulder, adding pressure so she backs up. I lower my knees to gain eye contact from the witness "That true?"

She looks around the bustling precinct then nods.

Guiding her to an interview room to give us some privacy, and hopefully make her less jittery, I tell her friend to take a seat outside. She opens her mouth to argue but I'm already closing the door on her.

"Take a seat… Miss?"

"Jade, just call me Jade." She lowers herself into a seat. I'll need more than that but for now I'll take it. It had to be Jade, right? God was playing with me, he had to be.

"Okay, Jade. I know you're scared right now but I want you to take a deep breath and explain why you're here."

Her hands clasp in front of her on the desk. "I was out back of Club Blue," she murmurs. "Scoring some coke." Shocker. This bitch doesn't think we can spot an addict.

"And?"

"I finished… paying for it." She squirmed, meaning she finished sucking his dick. "Then went back in but I had put my purse down when I was…" *On your knees*. This time I can't stop my eye roll. "Anyway, I went back for it and there was a guy." She gags, her hand going to her mouth.

I jump up to grab a trashcan from the corner of the room and hand it to her. She retches a few times, the blood vessels in her eyes popping. "He was standing over the guy I scored from, bashing his head in with a rock or something. I managed to run away. He didn't hear me, he was too into what he was doing."

"When was this?"

"A couple days ago. Monday I think."

She thinks? God, why do they pump their body with that junk, it completely distorts their reality.

"You sure this is what you saw, Jade? It would have been dark, and you were no doubt intoxicated. Had you taken any drugs prior?"

Her posture grows rigid. "I know what I fucking saw! HE KILLED HIM. His cum was still coating my mouth, that's how quick it was. He

empathy

must have been watching. He could have killed me!"

I leave her in the room, telling her I'll be back. Her friend jumps up when I open the interview room door. "She's going to be a while," I say.

She smacks her lips together, chewing on gum.

"Shit, I need to pick my kid up. Tell her I had to leave."

Ignoring her, I make my way to Lieutenant Nash's desk. "You better have coffee," he quips as I approach.

"Do I look like a waitress?"

He grins. "Not any I have had the pleasure of meeting, thank fuck. What's up?"

"I have a woman claiming she saw a murder out back of Club Blue. Do we have any reports to back that up?"

He taps his fingers over his keyboard. "I would know if we had. We did have a sexual assault there last night, but no murders."

He brings up a profile of a pretty brunette. "Mary Keys, reported someone forcing her into the toilet and violating her."

I grind my teeth. Sexual assault is a trigger for me. I'm such a contradiction. I hate scum who violate people in that way, yet I can kill, violating their right to live. "Any leads?"

He shakes his head. "Came at her from behind. What's this woman claiming to have seen?"

"A dealer bludgeoned out back in the alley."

His eyebrows rise. "Well, take Rossi and go check it out, but I'm sure someone would have come forward by now. That's a busy place."

The stale stench of beer hits me in the face as I pull the door open to Club Blue. The dark blue walls and mirrored bar make the empty space in-between feel even more cavernous and cold. The place is still; no music, no people.

"Hello!" I call, seeking any movement. A click and then squeaking of a door behind the bar sounds in the room and a blond guy appears with a crate of beer bottles. He jumps when he sees us, his eyes narrowing.

"Who the fuck are you?"

I flash my badge, giving a narrowed stare of my own. He rolls his eyes, but his shoulders have become rigid.

"You people have already questioned all the staff. These girls get drunk, become slutty then regret it and cry abuse," he spits.

I eat up the space between me and the bar, bringing my hands down harder than necessary. "We're not here for that. Someone reported a murder." I let that filter in to his brain for a few seconds, watching his posture stiffen more.

"Here?" he asks.

"That's what we want to know."

His hands came up in a surrender manner. "I don't know nothing about no murder."

"Do you have a back exit into the alley behind the club?"

He nods, pointing towards the back end of the establishment.

"Is this open when the club is open to customers?"

He shrugs. "People use it to go out and have a smoke."

I lift my chin towards the door for Rossi to follow and make my way over

"It fucking stinks of piss and sweat," Rossi says. I hate that I'm put with this idiot while my partner, Zach, is taking time off.

"You're in an alley at the back of a club. Just breathing down here we could pick up a disease." I notice a camera on the side of the building straight away. "Does that work?"

"Yeah," the bartender replies

"I'm going to need the tapes from as far back as you have them until today."

"You think this woman is legit?" Rossi asks, but it's muffled by his hand over his mouth. I shrug, going to the dumpster a few feet from the fire exit. I pull on some gloves and lift the lid, noticing how full it is.

"Find out what day the trash gets collected."

His footsteps carry away from me. The alley is wide, a good twelve feet, and fifty feet long with multiple back entries from the adjoining building. If someone did commit murder here, it would have

empathy

been spontaneous. No way would someone plan to murder here.

Lifting the lid on the last one, the smell of death and decomposing flesh seeps into my nostrils. I flip the lid over and lift a few bags. There's blood covering a body that rests at the bottom.

"Today. They collect the rubbish today," Rossi calls.

"Call CSI, we have a body. Looks like he's been here a few days so Monday night seems right, which means our forty eight hours before the trail runs cold is already chilly. I need you to canvas for witnesses, establish a correct time frame. You can get all that from the video tapes. We need motive and a suspect."

Rossi flips his phone out to make the call just as the bartender re-emerges.

"I need a list of the staff here and their roles. I want to know who's been putting out the trash. We need to get this crime scene secure before any more evidence gets contaminated. You'll need to keep the bar closed tonight."

He agrees, rushing back inside.

"I can still smell it." My eyes trail from the screen to Rossi who's holding up a pot of hand cream, inhaling it like it's a baked good.

"Stop being a pussy. Where did you get hand cream?"

His eyebrows almost touch his hairline. "It's my girlfriend's. I get dry hands from writing up paperwork all day, don't judge."

God, if he thinks I judge him on that alone he is wrong. The fact that he is useless and hates the smell and sight of the dead, yet became a homicide detective is so agitating I want to shove his face inside a dead body until he's used to it.

"Why do we have to do all this over a drug dealer?"

We've been going over the surveillance tapes for hours; I just came in to watch Monday night's. Fighting the urge to hit his head off the table I reply with incredulity, "It's a murder! We're homicide detectives. We investigate all homicides, Rossi. You can't pick and choose based on the identity of the victim. He also wasn't killed for being a drug dealer. It was random; he could have been anyone which means he may be the first victim with more to come." I drift off on the final word when a figure appears on the screen. He is wearing a black hoodie, pulled up to hide his face, and black track pants. The victim is trying to piss up against the wall after just leaving the witness. His lips are moving in the assailant's direction, making him stop in his tracks. The victim seems oblivious to the fact the assailant has scooped up a loose brick that was lying close to one of the adjoining buildings. He's completely blindsided to the harsh, vicious attack. One blow to the skull takes the victim to his knees, another knocks him unconscious, but he continues to brutally slaughter him with blow after blow, some to the face, others to the upper body. The video shows the back door open and quickly close, catching the attention of the murderer. He calmly stands, walks over to the trash crate, opens the lid and picks up the victim with ease, dropping him in before walking slowly away.

"That was fucking sick," Rossi says.

"He's done this before."

His eyes snap to me. "How do you know that?"

I tap the screen. "Any detective worth his badge can see it."

Chapter 15

Tail

Blake

WAITING OUT FORENSICS TO GIVE us a lead as the video didn't give us an I.D, and handing over the case to more experienced officers was against my better judgement, but Melody was consuming my thoughts and I had the assignment of tailing her. Who am I to disobey orders?

She looks tired, her face free of makeup, her long mocha swirled hair piled messily in one of those top knots students favour. She's been crying today; her eyes are puffy. She's wearing yoga pants, tight as fuck, like latex hugging her figure, and a tee tight over her generous chest, flaring slightly at her toned midriff. A pair of worn-in Chucks complete her attire. She's typing on a phone but her teeth are gritted.

I follow her, unseen, to a gym. I flash my badge to the receptionist to find out what she's signed up for. Self-defence, which makes me smile. This smiling shit is happening more often than I should allow it but she's taking control. She's adjusting and learning from the hand life has dealt her. When your story is written on a piece of paper and that paper gets crumpled up and thrown into a shredder, you can piece the tatters back together although the damage remains. So does your story, you just have to continue to write even if the paper isn't perfect.

Two hours pass before she emerges from the building. Night has claimed the sky, the moon full and proud standing in bright contrast against the darkness. She examines the sky, almost surprised night time has fallen, before her eyes dart around, her bottom lip disappearing into her mouth. She's nervous, her body tense as she begins her walk.

I follow her on foot, keeping my distance but she's more aware then I give her credit for because she senses me. Her legs pick up speed before she breaks into a sprint. I give chase, calling her name. I call her name four times before she slows to a stop, spinning to face me, her mouth agape. There's a mist of sweat coating her skin, and her chest is rising in heavy pants as she claws at the air to fill her lungs of oxygen.

"You're going to kill me," she breathes. My footing stutters making me falter and step back from her. "You keep scaring the crap out of me. You're going to give me a heart attack, I swear. What the hell is wrong with you?"

I take a step forward, gripping her shoulders forcing her back against the wall of the tall building she stopped in front of. Her eyes flare. This may be a shock for her, forward and without warning, but I need to taste her lips again. It's not something new for me, it's something that disturbs my dreams and occupies way too many of my thoughts. I need to sate the desire.

I crush my body against hers and enjoy her struggle as she tries to fight me off. *Good luck.* My lips claim hers without remorse. Her mumbled voice vibrates against my lips, she's not granting me access but I swipe my tongue out anyway, tasting her rejection. I grind my

empathy

cock into her pelvis, eliciting a whimper, her lips softening and opening for me. I release her shoulders and slide my hands into her hair, fisting two handfuls. Her arms wrap around my back, clawing at me, and one of her legs curls around my calf. Her body moulds against me, a soft mewing sound resonating from her; she can't get close enough. It's like she wants to melt into me, and fuck if I don't want to absorb every drop of her.

Our tongues duel and dance together in a battle of lust and anger; I hate that she's making me weak by wanting her, and she hates what type of man I am, yet the fire that smoulders between us is so hot it's impossible to tread out.

I pull back and glare down into her pools of green, desire oozes from them, saturating me in her need for release. I want to embrace it, I want to swim in the essence of her but I need to rein in my stupidity. I'm on the job, we're in public and she's so fucking young, and in reality, a threat to me. She is the daughter of a mark. She walked into a crime scene with me still in it. She became part of the underworld I dwell in. My hand has been tight around her neck; she wore my mark in the form of a bruise. Fuck, that's just making me harder; I need to shut my brain off.

"What the fuck are you doing walking around alone at night? Do we really need to go over the rape/murder conversation again?" I growl.

Her body stiffens and pulls from mine, her tiny fists pounding at my chest. An angry burst of mumbled profanities spill forth for a good two minutes before she lets up. Nose wrinkling at me, she huffs and waltzes off.

I swallow the impulse to knock her out, shove her in my car and throw her in her room for the night, and instead I jog to catch up to her. "I'm sorry… sort of." I wince when her angry glare penetrates me. "You need to be careful. You're reckless and it annoys me."

I stride a few feet in front of her before I realise she's stopped walking. Turning to face her hostile stance, I lift my hand to ask why she stopped.

A laugh without amusement bursts from her. "You are unbelievable. What the hell do you want? Why do you even care? Why are you here right now?"

Hmm fair point, the little brat. "It's my job to keep an eye on you," I tell her like it's obvious.

Her head jerks back, her mouth popping open. "What?"

I close the space, reaching for her wrist, my thumb stroking over her pulse. "You're in our jurisdiction now and believed to still be in danger so we have to keep you safe."

Her face crumbles, her eyes closing then springing back open; the jade pools glitter from unshed tears. "So you know."

I tilt my head to study her, to show her the softness she needs right now. I want to comfort her, take away the pain rippling through every fibre of her being. I'm mute, struggling to deal with these emotions crashing into me; it's like my feelings are waking up after being dormant. The rush confuses and terrifies me. I don't want to give them access but my system is being rebooted with a virus I don't have the firewall to protect myself from. It's just flooding in, seeping into my bones, my blood, my mind, my heart.

I find the anger quickly at the girl who is forcing this shit on me, and I hold onto it and anchor myself. "I know you witnessed evil, felt the nature of a beast wrap itself around you, and yet you must crave danger because here you are putting yourself at risk." I step into her, shadowing her frame with my own. Tears leak free running a delicious trail down her tinted cheeks. "You don't need to go looking for it. It's looking at you."

She pulls her hand free from me. "You're a bastard."

A chuckle, dark and deep, pulls from my chest. "Best you remember that, Puya."

Narrowed jade irises pin me to the spot. "Puya?"

I nod in the direction of her wrist. She turns it to look at the tattoo there. Shaking her head she starts to speak "It's a moonflower, a…"

Night-blooming cereus, I know," I finish for her, annoyed by her assumption I'm stupid and couldn't tell. In reality I'd fucking Googled it when I saw her tattoo and learned a whole lot about rare blooming flowers. I internally cringe at the lengths I've gone to find out everything about her. Googling her tattoo? I'm worse than a woman. I seriously need to whip out my junk and check I still have any. "But it should be Puya. Now get in my car."

Her hand drops. "No!"

empathy

I rush her, bending, my shoulder connecting with her midriff as I lift her over my shoulder, my arm wrapping around her thighs to steady her. Her breath disperses against my back in hot puffs as she struggles from the fireman's hold.

"Oh my God, put me down. This is police harassment."

A genuine laugh splinters the air. Shit, she's funny but her squirming is making me rethink not knocking her out. Her obvious arousal from our make out is so close to my mouth I can smell her scent and it's so divine my teeth bite down on her upper thigh. Her squeal then heavy breaths tell me I shocked her but also turned her on.

"Stop moving or I'll bite harder," I warn, hoping she'll wiggle her body all over me.

I reach the car and lower her to her feet. I pull open the door and gesture for her to get in. When she doesn't move I grasp her head and push down and back like I would a perp, forcing her into the car. I wait for her to drag in her feet before I slam the door, making her flinch.

I enter the driver's side, holding up my hand when she goes to speak. "Listen Melody, I don't like this shit any more than you do. Trailing some chick looking for danger is not my idea of fun." Her mouth does that popping open thing again, forming an O. "I don't like you and you don't like me but hey, here we are, so stop being a brat and we'll get along just fine."

I reach for the button on the radio, cranking the volume to drown out any comeback she fires at me.

She barely lets me stop the car before she jumps out and races into her dorm. I bite back the unsettling feeling of seeing Ryan sitting on her steps waiting for her. I drive away before I have to watch him go inside with her.

Chapter 16

Games

Ryan

MELODY DIDN'T MAKE IT TO class so she will miss out on the little show I've orchestrated. I'd slipped into the locker room and nabbed Clive's sweatshirt last week, and now it is in Jacob's bag. I've been waiting, drilling a hole in the back of his head, sending willing thoughts to him to open his bag. My call is answered when Clive asks him for a pen.

"What the…?" Jacob says when he opens his bag in front of the entire room and the "missing" sweatshirt is there.

My blood buzzes in my veins. It's fun to watch when plans play

empathy

out perfectly.

"That's my missing sweatshirt, dude!" Clive grabs it from a confused Jacob. Hmmm... wait for it. "What the fuck!"

Jacob looks over to see what he's talking about.

"Eww, is that jizz?" the guy sitting to his left asks.

Jacob's eyes widen and flick to Clive. Clive leaps from his seat, throwing the offending item at Jacob who lifts it to his nose to smell it, then throws it to the floor when he confirms that it is, in fact, cum.

"Clive wait," he calls, racing to catch up.

"BACK OFF!" comes Clive's rumbling reply, all eyes wide and on the show they put on for us. Sean nervously bites at the skin around his nails. Hushed tones hum throughout the room.

Weak and so easy to manipulate. This was way too easy.

Chapter 17

Changed

Melody

SHOPPING GIVES ME A REPRIEVE. Red and Cherry are fun and easy to be around, but a lot to take in huge doses. The self-defence classes give me a small outlet for my anger. Ryan's presence is comforting. I need his friendship, I need something to cling on to, but I only ever completely let go and drown in nightmares. The only time I grasp something tangible is when I run into Blake, the grating, self-absorbed, infuriating but totally gorgeous douche bag. I'm insane, I must be. Every thought of him leads me to fantasizing about him taking me, and when I'm around him, God, I lose all ability to ward off my

empathy

vagina's impulses; she wants him, not me, and that's tough luck for her because he quite clearly stated his hate for me. Why did he kiss me? Damn it, I need to forget about him. He's Ryan's brother, a detective doing a job, and a complete ass!

Over a week has passed since he kissed me but I feel him watching me, and see him on occasion, but he keeps his distance and that's fine by me.

I'm walking the halls, debating whether to go to class. It's completely irreversible, the act of evil, even if the sinner repents, the damage is done. I have been changed, shaped into a completely different person. I can't do basic things like looking in the mirror or eating certain foods, but it's the big things too. Dreams I once had don't feel like mine anymore, the choices I made feel like someone else's. I was re-born in the wake of my parents' slaughter, a new person harboring the tortured soul of the girl who died with them that day.

"Melody." I turn to the call of my name. Mrs Rhodes is approaching me, a smile plastered on her face. Her sleek blonde bob shapes her sharp jawline. Small, black framed glasses sit low on her nose; her brown eyes appraise me over the top of them. "You missed our session."

I force a small smile. "I told you, I don't need counseling."

The tilt of her head makes me want to flee from her pity. "You were a victim of a terrible crime. Anyone would need counseling after that."

Her hand comes out to rest on my shoulder. I've been touched this way too many times since it happened, and each one felt as hollow and lonely as the next.

I lift her hand from my shoulder and slip by her. I ignore her calling after me. I need to find Ryan.

Chapter 18

Family and friends

Ryan

MY DAY STARTED OFF BAD and the itch inside me burns to be scratched. Hunter Hartley, the waste of sperm who dipped his dick in my mother, making her conceive my brother, sent another letter to Blake; well, to Damian. The letter tells him about siblings he has. He wants them all to get to know each other. This man, after nearly twenty-six years, has the balls to try and take what isn't his.

I don't love Blake, but I like to claim ownership over things, and Blake is one of them. I like that he's alone like me. Being this hollow can be lonely. I put the new letter with the first, hidden in my room so

empathy

Blake won't ever have to betray what we are by embracing a family outside of me. The anger that festers from getting that letter makes me late again and brings me here, overhearing Clive telling some of the guys on the football team that he'll be sealing the deal with Melody soon. I choke on my bottle of water. This guy doesn't give up easy, and he's a nice distraction. He and Jacob have moved on from the cum on his shirt, much to my distain, but there are other ways to play that idiot. Melody texts me to see where I am, which gives me the perfect opportunity to show Clive up in front of his friends, a compulsion not to be quashed.

Five minutes after telling her where to meet me, she hurtles towards me, hair flying loose behind her like a cape. She's upset and looking for a friend to confide in no doubt, and I want to listen to all that anger and hurt bubbling on the surface of her façade, but the collective mumbles of Clive and his friends gaining distance forces my hand.

As soon as she's in reach, I grab her and kiss her, stunning her into accepting my advance. I hear the jibes and whistles from the football players as they pass us. It's the, *"Yeah, seems like there's a line and he's sealing that deal before you, Clive,"* that makes the ass grab and tit grope worth distressing Melody. I release her lips when I know they're out of hearing range. Her cheeks have Colored into a rosy pink. Biting on her lip with a dip in her brow tells me she's searching for the right words to convey what she feels. I see Sean's blond hair in my peripheral view but I don't turn. I just don't care enough to give a shit, as callous as that is. I can't find any reason or desire to make him feel okay. I didn't ask him to fall for me. Yes, I'm well above average in looks and intelligence but I can't help but wonder how broken these people must be to see something in me worth loving or wanting. I can't fucking stand most people; I want to take an axe to their skulls, peak in and explore what's inside. I almost feel sorry for Sean… almost. His hurt only fuels my desire to mock and taunt him. Use the feelings he concealed for me against him in the cruellest way possible.

The dark red mist of hell that lives inside me is becoming thicker, more demanding lately and I yearn to answer the call from within me. Feed the hunger, satisfy the cravings for malice.

"You're my only true friend here and I just don't feel that way about you, and I don't think you do either, right?" Melody looks up at me, longing for me to agree and although it's true, I felt no pleasure in that kiss, it still scratches at my ego. How fucking dare she reject me after flaunting herself at me, letting a friendship build? I see boy/girl friendships but those people are kidding themselves, ask anyone who has a close friendship with the opposite sex. One is either harboring feelings for the other, or they've fucked, kissed or fondled in the past. The only friendships between male and female that are platonic are those of friends' partners or a gay best friend. We were designed to mate, designed to fuck the opposite sex and when all is said and done, we always become stripped back to that.

I could destroy us here, be mean, embrace the beast and shred her with my toxic tongue. *"I couldn't get hard for that stench trench you're packing between those lumpy tree trunk thighs even if you showered the cock socket in disinfectant. The only thing that meat flap is good for is a hand warmer."*

I inhale and swallow the retort, and instead offer a relieved laugh, perfected over the years to convey normalcy inside me that doesn't exist. "Right. I had to make sure though. We could be great together otherwise."

Closing her eyes and then smiling, she hugs me. "We *are* great together. You're my best friend, Ryan." She sounds embarrassed to admit that we've known each other for such a small amount of time but she's so alone she would consider me her best friend. God, I would pity her if I could.

"I have that barbeque tomorrow. You still coming?"

She releases me with a squeeze and a nod of her head. "Yeah, sounds good."

"So, why did you look like you were ready to take on the world or cry just now?"

The halls have fallen silent. There are a few people milling around but most people have classes, including me and her. She shakes her head and shrugs her shoulders. "I just hate how people who don't know me assume they do and know what's best for me. No one knows this me." She's gone into her mind, her last words a whisper.

"You want to go grab coffee?"

empathy

The aroma is intoxicating. One thing I love is coffee. The machine behind the counter steams and sputters while the hot milk blends with two shots of expresso, filling the mug beneath it.

"Did you know coffee is a psychoactive? And at high doses it can make you see things. It can also kill you."

Melody claims us a table while the girl behind the counter tries to keep her eyes from me. She's attracted to me but has probably never spoken to a guy other than asking for his order. Her shy face lifts to glimpse at me, making sure I was talking to her. "It takes around a hundred cups to be fatal."

She hands me my order, slipping two biscuits on the saucer. "I'll cut you off at ninety nine, then," she quips, surprising me. I like her innocence. She turns from me and hurries away to make a waiting order.

"I'll cut you in half, spit roasting you, my cock one end and a twelve-inch double ended dildo the other, you virginal little bitch." My eyes close, reining in the temper boiling on the surface today. Her tense posture warns me she may have heard me over the chugging of the coffee maker. Her head turns sheepishly and I offer her my shit-eating grin and a head tilt as thanks for the coffees.

I find Melody sitting in the back of the shop, snug in a corner booth. I place her latte in front of her which she cradles like it's a lifeline. I slide in and just wait her out. I know she's getting ready to divulge something I will want to hear every detail of.

She inhales a shaky breath. "My parents are dead." She just blurts it out, like she's telling me it's raining outside. I bite down on my gum. My hand reaches over the table to take her hand, her eyes are focusing on something across the room but I know her mind is racing with memories. "Talk to me, Mel."

She must know I need more than that. She was going home to visit them so she knows I know it's a recent death.

"They were murdered. I found them and I've been struggling with it all, and the stupid guidance counsellor expects me to talk to her about it. But God, I can barely make it through the day trying to not think about the smell, the blood and the… the…" Her breathing has become unstable, her hand rattles in my grasp. "…and she wants me to talk about it. Like it's that simple." She's crying now, her free hand swiping angrily at tears.

"What did you feel, losing them like that?"

Her hand snatches from me. "What the hell, Ryan? How do you think it felt!?"

I tilt my head and pinch my brows to show pain. I alter my breathing to make my voice appear small and affected by grief. "I lost my dad when I was eleven. Me and Blake found him. He tripped down the stairs, broke his neck."

She leaps from her chair and cocoons me in her hold. Sharing grief solidifies a bond, I see.

Chapter 19

Sharing

Melody

I CAN'T BELIEVE I AGREED to go to this barbeque. Ryan is picking me up any minute and I'm still standing here in my panties and bra, staring at a dress and an alternative jeans and a tee. It's hot today though; the heat pours through the blinds making my dorm feel like a furnace so the dress is the obvious choice.

I feel a little lighter today. I think sharing with Ryan helped me. The fact he has lived with the death of a parent too is a weird comfort. Granted, his dad wasn't murdered but he was still robbed of a person who gave him life, who raised him until his passing.

Maybe I'm not a lost cause after all. Ryan and Blake survived

My phone buzzes, startling me. It's Markus again, he won't leave me alone. Our family lawyer is finally home from his vacation and wants to have the will read but I don't feel ready to break up everything my parents owned, including the house and business. What will happen to all of that? God, I need to get it over with. Someone my age shouldn't be thinking about this stuff, but caving into myself and hiding from it isn't helping me. The shadows were creeping out from the dark and soon I would be completely lost amongst them never to find the light again.

"Melody." Ryan's voice booms through my door, making my heart almost explode in fright.

"Okay, I'm ready." I toss the sun dress over my head, grabbing my bag and slipping on some beige cowboy boots.

We pass Cherry and Red on our way out. They blush which, with their genes, lights them both up like beacons. They giggle and hiss at me to call them later, no doubt making assumptions again. If only they knew it was his older brother's lips I've been attached to in the past and every night in my dreams since. Will he be there? Hell, of course he will, lots of detectives will be. Will they know who I am? Will they know what happened? Anxiety pumps the blood too fast in my veins. I feel a wave of unbalance followed by nausea flutter through me, bringing a chilled flush.

"They're just people, Melody. We won't stay long. We bailed on the last one."

My battle is clearly not just internal if Ryan senses my unease.

Blake

I DIDN'T BUY IT FOR one second when they arrested the drug dealer's roommate when he was trying to flee with his pal's drug haul. I've been going over the notes even though it isn't my case, but having someone that isn't me capable of such violence is a little too close to home. Ryan has been at the club many times and that murderer picked

empathy

his victim on a whim, I just know it. He was too brazen for my liking.

"What's that?" Ryan asks, walking into my office. I must have left the door open which isn't like me. Damn, I'm all over the place lately. I'm obsessed with Melody's brother and I keep going over the details, quelling the need to go confront him and wring his weak little neck. Her fucking eyes still awake me every night when they penetrate my dreams, my cock hardens and demands I relieve it as my mind relives her hot little mouth on mine, and now this case is niggling at me.

"Blake!"

I snap my attention to his risen voice. "Sorry. What?"

He lifts his chin in the direction of the photos and report on my desk.

"Oh, it's work. Did you hear about the murder at Club Blue?"

"Of course, everyone has. The paper claims they have a suspect. That true?"

I lean back in my chair, my hands coming up behind my head. "His roommate, but I don't buy it."

He stares at me intently; a lift of his lip almost gives into a smile. "That's because you're better at your job than those text book nerds. What do you care anyway? He was a bottom feeder."

I drop my arms, scoop up the files and slip them into one of the drawers. "It's my job, Ry." He scoffs, drawing my glare. "What the fuck's your problem?"

I keep all details of my other job/activities secret from Ryan; it isn't something he ever needs to know and if I ever fuck up and get caught, he can't be implicated. Knowledge is power, but ignorance is also power in these circumstances.

"No problem." He chuckles over his shoulder as he walks from the room.

"Ryan! Stay out of this room."

"Whatever."

I hate being at little events like this, surrounded by happy people, all friendly and engaging. I'm not the only one faking my smile. Suzanne's smiling right now at Mike's wife, Courtney, while inside she despises her for being the one he married when she has been in love with him since high school. Mike is sharing a beer with Mary's husband, and later will be fucking Mary in one of the many bathrooms this place boasts. I'm not against having laughs, I actually like some of the officers I work with. My partner, Zach, is as close to a best friend as I allow myself since high school. Jasper was my best friend back then, when I allowed myself to have normal relationships like friendships, but he moved away for college and never came back. He's settled down, got himself a husband and a wife if the rumors are true. Good for him.

I need to get laid. It's been too long and I get trigger happy when I'm on the edge. Sex is a good release and I need to do anything to stop myself thinking or watching Melody. Damn, that woman has crawled under the surface into layers I didn't even know I had. It's confusing and I hate the unease inside me. I'm used to a slightly simmering calm on the surface of my façade while I bury any type of emotion and live with an indifferent quality to life. The only thing is, now I realise it's just a way of concealing emotions I still own. If the way she made me feel is any indication, my emotions are becoming unburied and I hate her for making me notice this. I hate her for making me feel this way. I've never felt this before, how is she doing it? I just need to get laid, maybe that will wane whatever the fuck this is, because hate and lust are the only emotions I own up to feeling, so I'll just hate fuck everything else out of me.

I check my watch to see how long I've been here.

"Not even an hour, don't even think about it! You're helping with the grill." Zach glares, handing me a beer. Shit, that bastard knows me better than I thought.

"I need to get laid." I groan, looking over at Jess wearing a summer dress that barely covers her ass. She has all the right equipment but my dick just isn't up for playing with it. The noise grows boisterous with greetings. I look over and nearly spit out my beer; Ryan is here with her. Her LIVE tattoo is accompanied by a night blooming cereus but she doesn't just blossom in the moonlight, she looks just as

empathy

stunning under the beam of the sun. It embraces her in its glow, the flecks of red glimmering from its touch.

I stand, walking up behind them, overhearing Mills asking how long they've been a couple.

"We're just friends," Melody answers, her feet shifting. The shit-eating grin from Mills could have eclipsed the sun, it's so big. His head tips back to let the "ha" rip free.

"You can't win them all! Ryan, that has to be a first. Your pretty boy looks didn't get a girl wet for you, huh?" Mills has been necking the booze, and he's obviously well on his way to being wasted and punched out if he keeps letting his mouth run. Ryan studies him for a few seconds before turning to a red-faced Melody. As if in slow motion his hand moves up towards her, impacting her shoulder, causing her footing to stutter and her arms to flay wildly. Her body tips backwards and her mouth pops open, a little screech gaining everyone's attention. She crashes, breaking the surface of the water in the pool, the splash small, raining down to puncture the undisturbed calm around her.

"I can still get her wet."

There's no joking, no remorse for humiliating and soaking his friend in front of everyone. Jess sniggers but mostly there are gasps and muffled words of disapproval.

Her little gasps for air when she surfaces make me want to lick the water from every inch of her skin to elicit gasps of pleasure. Zach holds his hand out to her, pulling her from the water. His wife, Jasmine, is already holding a towel out to her, whispering where she can dry off and find something to change into. She scurries away, her eyes downcast.

Gripping Ryan by the back of the neck, I pull him away from the rest of the gathered crowd. "What the fuck was that?"

"He forced my hand by being a prick, and what do you care anyway?"

His pride, that's why he humiliated her.

"I'm an asshole, Ry, but even I can see that was shitty. You don't keep people around, but this girl, you have don't push her away over some asshole taking a pot shot."

His onyx eyes glare back at me. "You're right. I'm going to fuck his wife's face and then apologise to Melody."

He pulls from my grip, leaving me gaping.

I answer the call from inside myself and go in search of Melody. I find her in the en-suite bathroom of the main bedroom. She's a sin to someone like me but the rush from just a taste is worth God's wrath, and let's face it, I'm not going to be in the queue at the pearly gates; I'll have a ticket straight down.

"Oh God, you!Stop doing that shit, you're like a ninja!" She gasps, trying to catch her breath. I growl at her in response. I'm sick of seeing that face in my dreams, those pouty fucking lips, those green orbs burrowing to unlock shit inside me that had no business being unlocked.

"What the fuck are you doing here?"

Her little gasp makes my cock even harder; it's pushing against the seam in my jeans, putting pressure there and craving release.

"I'm with your brother, he invited me."

Shit, hearing that, even though I already know makes my temper boil. I hate that I want her and I hated that my brother has been getting her in some way or another. Her time spent with him makes me… holy shit… jealous. I'm acting like a teenage girl with a crush. I need her to hand my balls back. She's playing a game, she has to be. How she got Ryan to keep her around intrigues me but not as much as the fact she let me touch her and then spent all her time with him. That pisses me off. It's unusual for him to keep people around. I've never seen him care about anyone, not even me.

Damn, I need to get out of this small space. I'm too close to her. Her body is giving off signals and she doesn't even know it. Her nipples are hard, pushing against the flimsy fabric of her dress. Her eyes glaze with lust, she wants me, and I could take her, just a taste, right now.

"Did you want something else or are you just stopping by to show me you're still an asshole?"

I can't contain the laugh that tears from my chest. "You're brave, I give you that." I observe her, stepping closer.

She battles with herself. She doesn't want to show her wariness but the tiny step back and her pupils expanding tell me she knows better than to not be. Fuck, her little frame shakes, beads of water soaking

empathy

into her skin. Her damp hair clings to the side of her face; her bottom lip edible as it trembles, enticing me to take her.

"Is your appearance all part of your trap, Puya? You must be a wild lay to keep Ryan coming back for more. He's a little twisted, even for my tastes. Your pussy must grab like a vice."

I'm just provoking her. I know it isn't like that between them. Lust turns to hate in a flash, all telling in those expressive eyes of hers. Her hand twitches before she raises it and connects with my cheek, but I don't want to stop her. I want to feel a little something, anything to stop me doing something worse.

"You're so fucking vile. Who broke you? Who made you so hateful? Because that's where you should target your bitterness, not at everyone else."

I would have laughed if I didn't feel the truth of what she said so deeply. "You can talk."

Her body straightens and her eyes explore mine. "My world became disjointed but I keep the hate for the target inside until I know where to aim it. I don't shower it on you, so stop drenching me in yours."

Her tiny shoulder nudges mine for me to move and let her leave. I push her back, her balance giving way from the force, her butt hitting the side of the bath. She looks up at me as I tower over her. "What are you doing?"

Her breathing is heavy and totally betrays her need for what I'm about to do. I jolt her legs apart with my knee. Her thighs quiver against mine. I drop to my knees and her eyes wildly explore my face. I push my upper body between her now spread legs, scraping my hands up her damp, slick thighs, leaving red trails from my fingertips, forcing her dress to rise. Her chest rises in rhythm with my own erratic heartbeat. The desire emanating from us is almost palpable. Every further inch I uncover makes me harder. Her white cotton panties come into view, her pussy almost visible against the soaked fabric. Ryan is a dick for what he did but, God, I want to thank him in this moment. She leans back, showing she wants me to continue, her arm braced on the tiled wall behind her, the other grasping the sink. I slowly dip my fingers into the lip of her panties and drag them down a couple of inches, just until her bare mound is exposed. Saliva floods my mouth, and leaning forward I grip her hips and tug her to my lips, sucking her mound into my mouth, biting her there.

"Oh my God."

I jolt when the moan doesn't belong to her; her body has stiffened. My eyes collide with her urgent green swirls. The noises are coming from outside the on suite bathroom we are in. Someone's come into the adjoining bedroom.

"Get on your fucking knees." Shit, it's Ryan. I lift my finger to my lips, miming for her to keep silent. With a nod, her bottom lip disappears into her mouth. God, she's making me not think rationally.

"You wanted it, take it all the way, you filthy fucking whore."

My eyes close as Melody's eyes nearly pop from their sockets. A slapping sound then gurgling follows. I slowly rise to my knees, backing away from her exposed treats with remorse. She furiously straightens her clothing, trying to be quiet, and flinching when her dress, heavy from being wet, slaps against her skin.

"Choke on my cock, bitch, then go kiss that cunt of a husband."

"Shit, don't say things like that. It's not sexy."

My jaw tightens and my fists open and close. Mills' wife. He wasn't kidding. This little shit is going to bring real trouble down on him with this crap and I'll have to bail him out and still work with these fuckers.

I risk a quick glimpse, and sure enough Mills' wife is bowed beneath Ryan, looking up, worshipful. Fucking cradle-robbing whore. This woman doesn't give a shit that Ryan is a nineteen-year-old kid dealing with crap that happened to him as a child the only way he knows.

He slaps her across the face with his dick. "I'm not here to fucking woo you! Fucking shut your mouth unless you're eating my cock." He rams his dick down her throat, making her eyes water.

Light flashes. "Smile for the camera."

She tries to pull away but his other hand holds her firmly against his dick, forcing her onto him. Her nose is almost touching his pubic bone, her head is shaking, her hands wildly slapping at his legs. He's laughing, looking down at her and taking evidence on his phone.

Shit. I don't want to make my presence known but she's going to pass out if I don't.

empathy

"Ryan!"

His hand releases her on reflex. She falls backwards on to her ass, gasping for air, tears streaming from her bloodshot eyes. "You…. bastard!"

I point at her. "You're a fucking slut. Get out before I tell your husband what a whore he married." Her eyes drop to the floor. She gets to her feet and races from the room. "Ryan, what the actual fuck?"

He slips his dick away, buttoning his fly. "I told you what I was going to do. You seen Melody?"

"No, I haven't seen her," I grate out, and watch in astonishment as he leaves the room as if what he did is perfectly normal

"I think I'm just going to leave," Melody whispers from behind me.

"I think that's a good idea and it gives me an excuse to leave too. I'll drive you. Being here is excruciating."

She scoffs and flees the room.

Melody doesn't even say goodbye to anyone. I find her walking up the street in her wet clothes. She looks ridiculous.

"Get in the fucking car now. You're making a spectacle of yourself and it's embarrassing."

Fury pours from her. "Drop dead, Blake."

Grabbing her hips from behind to halt her, I repeat, "Get in the fucking car!"

"Fine! But don't touch me, asshole."

Ha! She loves me touching her, the deluded little brat. "My brother just made my dick shrivel up and die so don't worry your pretty, lying little head, princess."

She slams the car door, yanking at her seat belt "Lying?"

"Yeah, lying. You fucking love me touching you, Puya, you can deny it with these lips," I stroke a finger over her gaping mouth, "but those lips…" I wink down at the feverish junction between her luscious thighs, "divulge your lies." I smirk at her. "Shit, it's throbbing right now, isn't it? Creaming from the anticipation." Her gasp is audible. "Well, hold it in, Puya. I couldn't get it up now if I tried." That's a lie and I hope she won't look down and mock me for the same shit I just spun at her.

Complete silence descends and lasts the entire drive home. I pull up to her dorm.

"You're welcome." I grin at her hostile posture.

"I hate you."

"No, you hate yourself because you don't hate me." I know because I hate me for the exact same thing. I don't voice the last part though.

She darts from the car and I wait for her to disappear behind the closed door before driving home.

Chapter 20

Storm

Blake

ANOTHER JOB HAS COME IN, but ever since her I've questioned my life choices. How many young girls like her are out there living with actions caused by my hate for what happened to us? Was I reckless with the jobs I accepted? The half-brother claimed the father was volatile towards women and the mother was a spectator in his perversions. With my own blind hate for my parents I conceded this warranted the death penalty. I should have investigated further, but the truth is, I knew how under the radar these crimes can be. No one knew how abusive our father and mother were so who was I to question this guy?

There has to be a desperate reason to want to kill your father, right? Turns out greed can be a good motivator for murder. Their lawyer is home now and the will will be read, giving him a nice surprise which has the detectives investigating the parents' murder and looking more closely into Markus. I'm not worried, our communications were very secure and the only evidence of them is from me printing the details out to go over them with a fine tooth comb after that night.

My phone buzzes, breaking into my thoughts. It's Ryan. "Hey, you still at the barbeque?" I ask.

"Nah, I left shortly after you. I just called Melody. She called me an asshole."

"You are an asshole."

"She's being a moody bitch; it's her go to attitude lately. Anyway I called because I can't find my wallet. Did I leave it on the kitchen table?"

"Yeah. Where are you?"

"At her dorm."

Swallowing the primal growl crawling up my throat I tell him I'll bring it to him.

I pull up next to Ryan, stunned by the sudden turn in weather. Rain pelts down with such force it blurs the scenery through the windshield, moulding it all together into a distortion of colors. I lower my passenger window to see Ryan standing under a shelter, staring across the road. I try calling to him but he's engrossed in whatever has his attention. I slam my hand down on the steering wheel and look over at the back seat to see if, by magic, a jacket has appeared there. No such luck. I grab his wallet and make a dash for it. The pellets hit me like thousands of tiny needles, the air is still thick despite the beckoning storm, and a flash of lightning ignites the sky shortly followed by an eruption of thunder.

"Ryan! What are looking at?"

I follow his line of vision, my breath catching when I see Melody standing in the downpour, no coat. She's lost in the deadly grips of grief, her body shivering.

"She's broken. Fuck, Ryan. She's crying, what are you doing?"

His eyes reluctantly drag from her to me. "Watching."

empathy

She's breaking inside, the fragile pieces coming away with the water as it pours down on her. Her sorrow is so tangible it's as if her pain summoned the storm.

I slap his wallet against his chest and run to her. I have to. I may be a sinner but I don't want her to hurt. I want to wrap her in a sheath of my strength, give her something to hold onto. I want to share her pain so she doesn't ever cry like this again. If I could crawl into her mind and erase the terror she witnessed, I would. I'm gone, this is it. Seeing her helpless, her soul on the verge of disappearing into the storm, shifts everything I've been hiding from into focus.

Chapter 21

Emotions

Melody

I BURST THROUGH THE DOOR, the rain beating against my skin, the cold droplets soaking me through but not cleansing the pain away. Loneliness is suffocating me. I miss my parents so much I can barely breathe. There are no leads but the police are releasing the bodies to us so they can be buried. It's a surreal moment, like learning they're dead all over again. My heart hurts so much. How can people survive loss like this?

The laughter of a couple running to find shelter is so deafening I want to scream at them to notice they have each other; they're happy

empathy

and completely oblivious to the person dying right in front of them. *I'm here, can you see me?* On the inside I'm screaming from the depths of this empty void but on the outside my pain is clearly invisible because no way could people ignore the death of a soul happening in front of them, right?

A shiver rocks me, making my whole body vibrate. I stand, drenched, my clothes sticking to my skin but I can't move. The beats from the downpour tap dancing over the ground is keeping me from picturing them; it's grounding me to this moment. , the drops hitting the surface bouncing off expanding, swallowing, drowning everything beneath it. My tears blending with the coating of the rain. I want to cry out the hurt but there aren't enough tears to convey the pain, so powerful it leaves a physical ache surrounding my heart.

"Puya?" Blake, barely visible through the torrent, calls to me. Why is he standing there in the rain? His intensity shifts the air around us. My heart beats hard, reminding me it can feel more than just the pain. He affects me in a way that confuses and excites me. His strides eat up the ground between us.

"Why do you call me that?" I murmur, not sure if I'm dreaming him. The way my mind has been in a constant fog lately, I wouldn't be shocked if I suddenly awoke in my dorm alone.

Droplets form, pebbling over the smooth planes of his face and in his heavy soaked hair before running a path down his beautiful features. Trickles cling to his long, dark eyelashes. He reaches out to me, capturing my wrist, the pad of his thumb stroking over my small tattoo there. "Do you want to die?"

The laugh ripples through me. What a question. I think I have died; I'm living between the two realms. His eyes bore into mine, my laugh turning quickly into sob, my hands trying to cover my face from his probing stare. My legs are weak; I'm going to fall in a heap right in front of him, all my scars on display for him to recoil from. Who could deal with someone grieving, losing themselves, drowning in the current of sorrow right in front of them, getting them caught in the wake of my despair?

Strong arms wrap around me, lifting me into a bridal hold. I can't look up at him. I reach my arms around his neck and burrow my face into the crook. I need someone to catch my tears, to just hold me and let me know I'm still here.

I don't query why he knows my dorm room as he opens the door and carries me inside, going straight to my bathroom. My eyes are still closed, and I hear the shower start and his heavy breathing as he manoeuvres us around. His heart thumps erratically against my chest and the warmth from the water makes me sigh as it pours over us, both still fully clothed. He lowers us into a sitting position in the cubicle with me on his lap.

"I'm so lonely without them," I murmur into his neck before lifting my head to find an intensity so raw in his eyes it flays me, stripping back the final layers, exposing my soul to him. "I need justice for them but I'm not going to get it… so I want vengeance, but first I want to forget for just a little while."

My breaths become yearning gasps. I need to feel something else. I need to feel connected. I can't keep dying alone, fading into nothing. I need an anchor.

My eyes drop to his lips. I feel his already hard cock beneath my ass. "Take me, Blake. Make me forget for just a little while. Make me feel something more than the hollowness."

His lips clash with mine, hard and merciless, his teeth nipping at my bottom lip, his hand slipping up into my hair, grasping fistfuls, tipping my head back with force. The build is already catching fire inside my core. He spins me so my back is against his chest, my ass sitting snugly on top of his hard erection. He tugs my hair, wrenching my head to the side so he can claim my neck, his lips sucking, teasing me. My hips grind against him to gain some friction to ease the ache throbbing between my legs.

His hands grip my wet tee, ripping it from my body, making me gasp and exposing my lace bra covering my hard, aching nipples. Reaching for the buttons on my jeans he tugs them open before I feel the warm, solid presence of his body leave mine for a few seconds. He fumbles above me, but before I can turn to see what he's doing, the warm water stops falling down on us. I'm about to ask him until his hand wraps around my front, pulling me hard against him once more. He leans me back and slips the shower head into my panties. The warm water massages in waves of continuous ripples over my

empathy

sensitive lips, making me squirm.

"Open yourself up for me," he groans into my ear.

I'm nervous but so turned on. I need the relief he's offering. I push at my jeans and panties so they move further down my legs. The cold air mixed with the heated of the water makes me catch my breath. He hisses when I slip my fingers to my pussy, opening myself for his eyes to devour. His growl and roughness as he rips the cup of my bra away, making my pebbled bud harder, sends shock waves of adrenaline pulsing through me. I'm almost vibrating out of my skin. He moves the shower head to my now exposed clit and I quiver; the pressure is perfect and he holds it so his knuckle is stroking the delicate bundle of nerves, his other hand pinching my nipple. I can't take it, the pleasure is incredible and I lose myself to lust so powerful it takes possession of my body and mind.

I writhe against him, his cock prodding against my ass and lower back. He's thick and long. My needy moans, loud and shameless, bounce off the tiled walls. My hands explore myself as he does, the build intensifying, the flutter in my lower stomach, the pulsing inside as my inner walls grasp for relief.

"Slip your fingers inside. Show me how much you want me." His hungry growl rumbles into my ear.

I move my hand over his, then down to my opening, sinking two fingers inside myself. My walls grab greedily at me, the friction from everything all at once makes my body cry out with an orgasm like I've never experienced before, igniting inside me, lighting every nerve in its path and leaving a tingling tremor in its wake.

The warmth of my cum coats my fingers as I ride out every shudder. The shower moves away and Blake's hand grips my wrist, slipping my fingers free. I turn my head to watch in fascination as his tongue swipes out and then sucks my fingers into his mouth. The groan thunders through his body, reverberating against my back, his lids fluttering closed.

"You're so fucking pure and sweet." His lips collide angrily with mine, my own scent mixed with his exploding on my tongue. It's too much but not enough all at once, a contradiction in the perfect form. His movements are slow and the usual flood of embarrassment and anger at myself for being weak to his advances creep over me. His eyes are too probing.

I stand, awkwardly fumbling to untangle myself from our entwined bodies. I get to my feet, look down at him staring up at me, grab a towel and leave the bathroom.

Chapter 22

Heal

Blake

I SAVOR HER FLAVOR ON my tongue. She's as sweet as I thought she would be. Her writhing against me as she came was the sexiest thing I've ever seen but her armour is thickening back up, awaiting my change in mood like our other encounters, no doubt. I always turned on her after she succumbed to my advances in the past, but this time is different. I know it's more than that now. Ryan mentioned that she's been off, moody in classes. She's building walls and as much as I have them too, I don't want to let her hide behind any, I don't want her to lose herself any more than she already has.

I follow her into her room. "You're not alone, Melody."

Her glare doesn't help the ache in my cock. "I don't need your sympathy, Blake. I don't need anyone's."

I enclose myself around her; she's standing in front of the covered mirror, her wet hair dripping onto the carpet beneath her feet. She's only in the tiny towel she rushed to cover herself with when she came down from the bliss of her orgasm. She steps forward to try to put some distance between us but I refuse to allow it, placing my hands either side of her and the mirror.

"I don't give sympathy easily, Melody. In fact, it's a new emotion for me. I know you're hurting, and sympathy from anyone is them showing you they feel your pain, they share it with you, so you don't have to carry it alone." Her body tremors from the emotions taking control of her. "I'm going to help you. Let me show you don't need to fear mirrors."

Her breath hitches as I snatch away the towel; our reflections stare back at us from the now visible mirror. She's shaking her head but I need to show her how to find power in her weakness, in her fear. I reach up, wrapping my hand around her throat, making her eyes flare wide and her petite hands come up to pull mine away. I lean all my weight into her back, my one arm still placed on the wall stopping me from crushing her into the mirror. Her scent is firing off all my desires.

I lick the shell of her ear before whispering, "Own your fear, Puya. Replace it with pleasure." I bite down on the lobe then suck the sting away. She's still tense. I flick my eyes to hold hers in the refection.

"Get out of my room. I feel sick that I let you touch me," she spits.

The bite wounds me more than I expect, but I know it's a coping mechanism. She is so close to breaking that it turns to anger to prevent herself from rupturing into particles, never finding her way back again.

"You want someone to hurt because you're hurting. You want them to know what it's like to see what your eyes have witnessed just so you're not alone in the ache haunting you, the misery holding you hostage in that house. Look at yourself!" I growl, turning her face.

"No, get off me."

"Look at yourself."

Her eyes strike her own image. Tears well, collecting into small dams of sorrow before overflowing, spilling in tiny rivers down her cheeks.

"It's them starring back at me. It's the only thing left of them, the only thing left of the girl they raised and shaped to make it in the world. That girl, the one who crawled out and left this shell, died in that house with them yet her face stares back at me. My dad's eyes, Mom's cheekbones and nose." She shudders from the force of her sob.

"And it's beautiful and should be celebrated. They created a stunning, remarkable woman who is still here, Puya. She just needs to accept it and live with the changes in that girl. No-one is ever the same when evil visits, but how you let it sculpt and define you is the key to surviving it."

Liquid jade swirls pierce me. The warm, soft pressure of her body presses into me as she leans back. She loosens the towel, making it fall to the floor. I kick it away with my foot and drink in the sight of her completely laid bare to me, not just her naked frame but her soul, her heart, all there for my taking if I wish it, and God help me I want it. To take it would change me irrevocably, but to ignore it would be irredeemable. I need to let this saint wash away some of the bad in me, but doing so makes me a worse sinner, corrupting an angel, letting her fall for the damned. I'm enthralled by her, I need to claim her completely, teach her to embrace the new her, pour all my fucking want straight into her, possess her pleasure and heal her fear.

Her skin is still damp, varnishing her skin with a cool mist, and tiny goose bumps layer the soft flesh beneath them. My hand skims back down to her throat, feeling the wavering pulse underneath it.

"Own it," I breathe, kissing along her shoulder, licking the coating of water mixed with her unique flavor into my mouth. Her hands rise up to hold on to the forearm of the hand gently squeezing her neck.

"Own me," she murmurs.

I pull free from her, causing her to turn to watch me scatter my clothes to the floor until I'm mimicking her naked form. Her mouth pops open when her eyes bear down on my thick cock standing on salute for her. I reach for her, fisting a handful of her hair and manoeuvring her to the bed. Attacking her plump lips with my own; thrashing my tongue into her mouth, I establish my dominance over her. I tear away, leaving her panting. Spinning her and pushing her front down on the mattress, my body follows over hers, enveloping her with me. I keep my hand firm in her hair tugging her head back. Using my knee I shift it between her thighs and tap aggressively, forcing her to widen them. I groan as the sheen of her arousal coats her perfect pink slit, her pussy lips spread, giving me a sample of what's waiting to swallow my cock. God, she's like the perfect sex buffet, her tight little pussy a feast I can't wait to gorge on but first I need to help her restore what's broken in her, this nightmare haunting and owning her. As sick as it is, the entity that installed this fear was me and it will be me to help her overcome it. It doesn't matter in this moment; this feels too right to be all the wrong, my brain was whispering it was.

I trace the glaze of her pussy with the tips of my finger, dipping one inside her. The answering moan entices me to slip another finger inside the liquid heat, groaning when her walls clench greedily at me, coating them in a film of her essence. I push deeper then pull back, gliding in and out at a teasing pace, making her ass wriggle and push onto my hand. "Ride my fingers, Puya. Show me how bad you need it."

Rotating her hips, she gains friction, and she feels so good screwing my hand with abandon. Her pleasure cries are driving me insane, making me hand fuck her right back, stroking at her g-spot with every thrust forward. I know she's going to cum, I can feel the tightening of her pussy, the rippling of her muscles grasping for release, and I will give it to her. Slipping my fingers from her without warning I plunge my hard cock balls deep with such ferocity the bed shifts under the intensity of my entry. One hand tugs at her hair, the other grips her hip, pulling it against the onslaught of my cock invading every inch of her delicious, warm core. She consumes me, I can't get any deeper inside her yet I'll never be deep enough. We're joined in ecstasy but the connection is so much more than that. I'm high on her elixir and I never want to come down.

My pace is fast and hard and she matches me stroke for stroke, circling her hips every time my tip pushes her to her limit. A warm feeling trickles up my spine the pressure and pulling in my cock as my ball tightened. Leaning into her, I drop her hair and wrap her life in my palm once again. My pelvis still thrashes into her, my balls slapping against her ass. Her wet pussy draws me in with haste but her body stills from the position of my hand.

empathy

"You survived." I ram forward, hitting the bundle of nerves tucked up in the front of her vagina. Her breath is stolen by my grip as I force my hips brutally into her. "Own it, then he can't win," I grunt as her body tenses, her pussy squeezing my cock so tight I think it may stay inside her even when I pull free. Her body breaks into a heated frenzy of pleasure throes, and I release her throat so her vocal cords can echo her moans into the room. My own release rips from me with ribbons of cum flooding her inside.

Chapter 23

Changes

Melody

I'M COMPLETELY EXHAUSTED SEXUALLY, MENTALLY and emotionally. I have never felt this raw before but at the same time, safe and slowly healing. Sex has always been pleasant for me. Zane was a tender lover, sweet and caring, but God I never knew sex could feel like that. Blake is bigger than Zane by a good few inches but it was the passion, the intensity of our need that was new to me. He read my body as if he was created just for that, he played my pleasure, creating a flawless symphony and I'm sinking in his sinful allure, but I don't want to be saved. I want to be covered in everything he is. I'm cap-

empathy

tivated by the soul of this inconsistent, confusing, mesmerising man who just showed me I can be saved. I can fix some parts of me that I thought were lost. I will never fully recover but I will learn to keep breathing, healing, and surviving without them.

The delicate touch of his fingertips dancing over my skin makes me smile up at him. He took me twice more after the first time, taking his time to sate his sexual palate. The sore hum between my thighs reminds me of his complete ownership over my pleasure. "Why do you call me Puya?"

He recoils a little before saying, "Your tattoo. It's not the only rare blooming flower. Puya chilensis are rare, and their bloom is extremely rare, but when they do it's unique. They are adaptable and can survive almost anything."

I move further into him. "That's beautiful." His nose wrinkles, it's quick and he tries to hide it but his eyes are looking everywhere but at me. "Are you lying?" I prod at his naked chest. He grins and it's breath-taking.

"No. I'm avoiding a key element."

"Spill it."

Wrapping me up in his arms and pulling me on top of him, he nuzzles my neck. "Sheep become impaled on their sharp spikes. They die and the plant absorbs them." I tug away from him but he holds me firm. "You snared me in your captivating hold, you re-wakened me and you've slowly been absorbing my soul every night since."

Oh God, I'm falling hard and fast. I lower my lips to his, soaking in the fierceness of his touch. Knuckles rap against the door and break our connection. If it's Cherry and Red they will melt into a puddle at the sight of Blake naked in my bed.

"Just be quiet they'll go away." I chuckle.

"Mel, you in there?"

Oh my God, Zane? My insides squeeze. I expected to hear from him sooner but not a visit. An email or text at the least, a call at the most, but shit, he's at the door and I'm naked on top of a detective.

"Who's that?" Blake's deadly voice shocks me into action.

"Shit, shit." I jump from the bed, grabbing my robe and sheathing my body in the thin, cool silk fabric. I gather Blake's wet clothes and toss them in the bathroom as he appears behind me, me making me jump.

"Who is he?"

I push him towards the bathroom. "He's my oldest friend," I answer, shutting him in the bathroom and going to answer the incessant knocking.

The door whooshes open with a gentle tug, lifting the air up around me and making my hair fly across my face. Callous fingers scoop the strands, tucking them behind my ear. Bright blue eyes meet mine, along with a half-smile.

"I'm so sorry, baby. I was away with the team, my folks only just told me. I jumped a plane straight here."

Tears fall from my eyes as his arms encompass me in their familiar comfort. His smell reminds me of home, the feel of his ironed shirt against my cheek, warm from his body underneath. Zane always runs hot. His athletic body is constantly burning, making him warm to touch even in the harsh winter nights.

My tears leak onto the cotton.

"Let's go inside, Cereus."

My stomach drops. Shit, how am I going to play this? I need to get dressed, get Zane out of here and then text Blake.

Zane slowly motions me backwards.

"I just need to get dressed then we can go get coffee. You want to meet me outside in ten..." My words fade into a whisper when I realise Zane is staring over my shoulder.

Awkward. I inhale and trace his path with my own eyes. Blake stands in the bathroom doorway, arms braced against the top of the frame, his sun caressed skin pulling tight over all those defined muscles. He works out, I felt him inside my body, pumping into me, over me, skin on skin, touched and licked every groove yet he still leaves me lightheaded, staring. He's shameless, bold and I'm uncertain of his motives. Will he make a crude joke or is he establishing his place, letting Zane know I have someone now. Do I have someone? Yes, without a doubt for me. He's inside, consuming me. , I felt him in my veins, follicles, every tiny fibre he had infected and I wasn't looking to be cured. I welcomed the fever he brought on me.

Zane's eyes bounce from me to naked Blake.

"Blake, this is Zane from back home. Zane, please excuse Blake's nakedness, we got caught in the storm."

Blake's hands drop to his sides, his feet taking casual strides towards us, his arm coming around my waist, pulling me against him. "That's not why we're naked, though, huh? Baby." He emphasises the *baby*, and a chill races across my skin. He heard Zane call me baby.

Zane studies us both before saying, "You seem like a real decent guy and all, Blade, was it? But I came along way and it wasn't to see who had the bigger cock. I came to see my girl."

The atmosphere is so thick with animosity, a recollection of the taste of blood in the air fires off in my mind.

"Please don't do this," I say.

I feel Blake's fury and it's terrifying. My body shakes. Zane's voice calms my nerves with his next sentence.

"Hey, breathe, Mel. It's okay. I'm going to wait outside while you get dressed, okay?"

This is why I loved him; he's level-headed and knows me so well. I can't handle any violence or aggressive glares and barbs, especially not from two people I care about.

The door shuts quietly behind him. Sighing I turn to smack at Blake's chest. "That was pathetic."

"Your pussy is warm with my cum and you being called baby while wrapped up in another guys arms is insulting to me."

I want to strangle him. He's a being a douche but he's right. I hid him in the bathroom like I was caught doing something wrong. We're both adults, and me and Zane haven't been together in a long time.

"You're crude and an ass but you're right. I'm sorry."

He seemed stunned by my reaction. His eye flash wide a slither of a smile tilting the corner of his mouth. "Good, because this shit is new for me and I don't know how to deal with everything I'm feeling. I'm learning as I go but I know this much, Puya. I claimed you as mine today and there is nothing and no-one that will change that. That means I may act pathetic from time to time but believe me, that is tame compared to what my inner voice wants to do, so you keep yourself from other guys' arms and I'll keep from killing them."

Okay, wow. What do I say to that? Since I met him he's been like a tornado ripping through me, turbulent and unpredictable. Now I'm in the eye it's still scary, an eerie calm with all the chaos swirling on the outer edge. He's baring his soul to me, showing me a deeper part of himself. He isn't used to connecting and although he really needs to word things better and not act like a caveman, he's being vulnerable, opening himself up and that is a huge deal for him. I want to protect his vulnerability, shield him from exposing himself so he doesn't feel weak from it.

"He has been in my life a long time. We were high school sweethearts." His rigid posture makes me squirm. "But that was high school and I'm learning that what we had doesn't compare to what I'm supposed to feel when I'm with the right person."

He had risked opening up so it was my turn, and I needed to lighten the tense tic in his jaw. "And for the record, you win in the bigger cock department." I wink.

He charges me, tackling me to the bed, grinding his bigger cock into me. "Damn straight, B.A.B.Y. I'm all man, that's why. He's still a boy."

I giggle. "Does that make me still a girl?"

He growls, tugging open my wrap and exposing my body to him. "You're all woman. My woman."

A million lightning bugs ignite my insides and travel to my heart. It's such an overwhelming feeling to know that in my lost despair, when I fell, I wasn't met with the ground this time. This time I was caught by him.

Chapter 24

Tethers

Ryan

IT HAS BEEN THREE HOURS since he lifted her up and carried her away. I underestimated how well they're entwined. He became someone new in the moment she broke, just like all those years ago with me, he changed in a moment. Why aren't I programed like him, or him like me? How can he change like that? There was no impulse from me to go to her. Well, one to get a closer look at her completely destroyed. Nothing powered inside me to go rescue her. I relished in her destruction, watched and claimed it as a token.

She was stunning in her heartbreak, and then he waltzed in and stole it from me.

Rain eases into a cool mist before evaporating, leaving dew in the thick air. Storm clouds move across the sky, leaving a grey tint ever dispersing to the cool blue of the summer.

There she is, bounding out like a whole new person. It's literally as if she's Mother Nature, beckoning the weather with her emotions. A blond guy flanked by two red-headed girls look up at her as she goes to him. Blake appears next, wrapping her up in a display of possession. Kissing her, slapping her ass before leaving her with the other guy.

Have I fallen into a black hole? What the hell is happening? None of this is right. How dare they find comfort in each other? They each belong to me. I need to feel control. Everything is slipping between my fingers.

I pull out my phone and dial Sean, telling him I need to see him at my place.

Chapter 25

Old and New

Melody

ZANE SMILES AT ME OVER the table. "So, Cherry and Red," is all he says, his expression saying everything his words don't, making me chuckle.

"Yeah, they're intense." The steam from the coffee in front of me swirls on the surface in a warning I don't heed, burning the tip of my tongue.

"Always were impatient."

It's good to see him, he's exactly the same but everything is so different. The world has shifted, altering me from the girl who once lay in his arms and dreamed of nothing but being with him. Everything was so simple then.

We live in a moment that's so quickly taken, it's like it was never even ours. Time is borrowed; you need to capture everything you can before it's just a fleeting memory of someone you used to be. You say you'll never change, you promise nothing will change what you have but those aren't our choices. The world changes, circumstances change.

"I called your house." Zane pulls me from my musings; a shift in my stomach brings the unsettling void to widen. "Markus answered. What is he doing there, Mel?" He knows Markus and I have never been close and that my parents' relationship with him wasn't all roses and family dinners.

"He wants me to sell the house. I can't do that, so he's there waiting for me to decide what to do."

The tension stiffens both our postures. Zane always hated the way Markus treated me. His eyes wandered too much on me for a brother, especially when he held distaste for me most of the time.

"You don't need to sell the house. There's enough money. Why would he even care about the sale of the house?"

I hate that this is what my parents have come down to. How much money they left. I don't care about any of it. I would gladly give it all away if it meant just one more day with them.

"Greed, Zane. You know what he's like. The will is being read tomorrow so I will just buy his half of the house from him and he can be on his way."

Sipping his iced tea, his eyes collide with mine over the rim of the mug. "You think he'll really get half?"

This makes me uncomfortable. I can't help but fidget which is a tell of mine when I don't like the direction of conversation. If I didn't need to be there I would just ignore it all so it didn't cement the fact they were really never coming back. This is it. I'm on my own with everything they built. Money will never be something I need to earn on my own. I can retire before even starting. It's all wrong. I'm twenty years old and life is forcing me to accept I'm now an adult and have tough decisions ahead, with only me to make them.

"Do they have any suspects? Who would do something like this?"

empathy

Wasn't that the million dollar question? It doesn't make sense and the detectives trying to imply it was about me is cruel and untrue. Blake told me there was no evidence to back up that theory and I just need to accept it was the act of a heartless, reckless individual.

"Someone hateful and sick." Pushing back the emotions threatening to drown me again I look him over. "You look good, Z. How is college treating you?"

His smile is natural, lighting up his entire face. "It's really good. They think I could go pro. I have scouts interested already."

Of course he does. Zane is a doer. He's one of those people who is destined to be something big. The sports world will gain a real talent, but not just that, he's honest and has the good morals to become a spokesperson for kids to really look up to. He's the full package and I'm honoured to know him, and to share such a treasured past with him. He owns a piece of my heart. He was my first love, and although my racing heartbeat whenever Blake is near tells me that my first powerful love will decimate any love that came before it, he still owns that part of me, it was his to keep, locked away safe in memories and milestones of our youth.

"I love you, Z. Thank you for coming here, it means more than I can say."

Zane's chair scrapes backwards and his warm arms wrap around me. He lets me crash into him, he accepts the collision head on and will try to fix the mess and all the lonely empty days I spent feeling invisible in my pain. I hadn't tried to call him to give him a chance to know I'm suffering. This morning I was disintegrating into the storm and now I have not one, but two men enforcing the truth that I'm not completely alone. If I let myself see that, I didn't die that night with my parents. I left that house.

Chapter 26

Embedded

Blake

LEAVING HER TO SPEND TIME with her ex-boyfriend took strength. I thought the more distance I put between us, the more rational my brain would become, but no, she's inside me. Embedded in the fibres and planting roots. She hit me with enough force to render me incapable of thinking of anything but her. My ghosts keep creeping from the shadows, telling me she doesn't deserve my darkness to taint her light but it was my sins that led me to her in the first place. Fate has given me a glimmer of sunshine in a blackened sky, and after losing control of who I really am for so long, it makes me aware I've have been sleepwalking through my life, living out the nightmares of others. Life coated me in a sheen of anger and hate but it's washing away bit by bit and she's the water, cleansing me.

Questions bombard me, the choices I made, the impact of my cold front on Ryan. Had I done what was best for him? Had I been an acceptable kin to him? I know I messed us both up; he was so calm at times it was almost unnatural. He completely checks out, leaving just a warm body. I tried to ignore the unnerving atmosphere he can emanate. I'm not sure how he'll react to the idea of me and Melody. She's different for him, a friend. I don't think he has ever really had one before her, but she's different to me too. She's saving me and I want to save her. She's waking me up to a life I thought lost to me. I'm tired and lonely. I hate admitting that to myself. I don't want to feel all this, it would be easier if I didn't, but it's too strong to fight and too incredible to want to. Being inside her and actually wanting to make her fly, wanting to drive pleasure through her, bring her to the edge, make her live in a moment of pure bliss was a need more powerful than finding my own release. Making her feel safety in my arms rather than fear ignited a craving in me to make sure she's never afraid again.

I need to go pack a bag. I'm not letting her go home and face that house on her own, and if that brother of hers is there, she won't be safe around him. He is a greedy, unstable fuck. I want to take him out, she'll be safer without him still breathing, but her fragile mind can't handle another death.

Chapter 27

Tease

Melody

AFTER SEEING ZANE OFF, I go back to my dorm to find Blake waiting for me with a bag. He's going to drive me home. Having him to lean on transforms the full on dread of having to go home into a simmering, uncomfortable motion in my insides.

I've been staring at his profile as he drives for the last hour. He's a beautiful specimen. Rugged but soft, hard lines with stunning features. I was lucky to even catch his eye but I have and the usual to and fro of lust/hate has fizzled into a thick haze of ultimate lust and possibilities of where we could go.

Tightening his grip on the wheel while sneaking glimpses of me, his eyes drop to my exposed thighs in the sundress I'm wearing, causing my breathing to quicken. "Puya, don't distract the driver." His tone is lower than should be allowed.

My insides heat up. He completely depleted me of energy earlier with his sexploits yet my body is igniting for him again and I need the distraction he gives me. Placing one foot up on the dash, my sundress sliding up to expose my panties, I take a deep breath and summon my inner slut. "What if he's distracting me?" I ask, stroking my hand down my neck, seductively tracing a path down my collarbone then chest; down my cleavage, pushing the buttons away so he can see the flesh burning up for him.

The car swerves, making me screech. The brakes hit hard. Before I can determine what's happening, he's round at my door, yanking it open and dragging me through it. He takes me to the driver's side and pushes my head through the open window. I brace myself on my arms as my palms hit his seat, my pelvis pushing against the frame, my ass prone in the air.

I reach up onto my tiptoes to gain some stability.

"What the hell, Blake?" I cry out, but the gust of cool air kissing my now exposed skin from him lifting my dress and tearing my panties away has my pulse vibrating. His teeth clamp down on my ass cheek, the burn of pain followed by the lapping of his wet tongue is a contradiction in the pleasure it gives me.

His mouth drops lower, the warm swipe against my slit makes my hips buck, my arms struggling to keep me up. "Like to tease the driver, Puya?"

Oh God. Frenzied fingers enter me, the position I'm in gives him a direct target to the sweet spot that sends me spiralling into intoxicated pleasure. The ache from having him earlier is still there, eliciting a steady rhythm of pleasure and pain. The cars passing, the daylight making us visible to anyone who looks our way and the thrusting of those long delicious fingers followed with the flicking of his tongue over my clit has my core kindling a blaze that's getting ready to tear through me. His other hand slaps down hard on my ass cheeks before parting them, tracing the seam all the way up with his tongue.

My insides tighten with nerves and desire. I want to pull forward to stop him from going near the forbidden, but I'm completely at his mercy and he's showing me none. As much as I haven't ever thought about anal play, his tongue stroking me there gives me chills. Pressure puckers against the hole before his thumb breaches the muscle. His teeth scrape up my ass cheeks then his tongue leaves a heated path up my spine while his fingers and thumb fuck me punishingly.

My dress falls over my head, trapping my arms and face in pools of fabric. My inner walls clutch at him.

"Yeah, squeeze me, Puya." His deep growl rumbles against my back. My orgasm hits in a stream of rippling ecstasy. My hips are being pulled backwards; hands coming through the window to hold the dress in place over my face and arms. The cool air in contrast to the warmer air of the car hits my fevered flesh, dispersing over my exposed stomach and breasts. I shake my head, trying to make the material fall so I can breathe better, but he has other ideas. I hear his belt whip from his jeans and he fiddles with the fabric, gathering it against my wrists. The belt fastens them together, trapping me inside its confines.

Mumbling for him to release me becomes groans when his hands grip my ass cheeks, lifting me; my legs snaking around his waist, crossing my ankles to hold on. His hard cock pushes straight into me, my inner walls coated in my release he had just gifted me moments before.

The heaviness of his chest pushes against mine, trapping my body against the car. The power of his movements is going to leave bruises up my back and I don't care in the slightest. He fucks me like he hates me; hard, fast and without compassion. My heavy breaths heating the air imprisoned in my dress leave me lightheaded. I'm in a translucent state of euphoria. Every touch magnified by my senses being taken away. The fear and excitement of being seen, and the pure high of every jerk of his hips. I ride him right back, twisting my hips as much as he allows, gripping his cock, stroking every inch with my inner walls. I'm flying, my whole body vibrating with my release.

His warm sprays of cum glaze my already sensitive nerves, prolonging my climax. The ties at my wrists became lax, my dress falling back over me. Gasping at the fresh air, I can't take my eyes from his. Strands of my hair cling to my sweat-coated brow. I know I must look a mess but I'm humming all over and the way his eyes devour mine, I don't think I could ever feel unattractive in his presence.

"Don't tease the driver."

A giggle erupts from me, surprising him, his eyes widening. Hot, heavy palms grasp my face, dragging me to his lips, his tongue forcing entry to my mouth. I melt into his embrace, giving myself to his possessive need.

A tooting of a car horn makes reality swarm in. Embarrassment tinges my cheeks and mixed with the sex flush, my face is on fire.

"You have no clue how beautiful you are. How is that even possible?"

I'm not sure if he meant to voice his thoughts, but my internal organs are ready to combust with how many feelings rush through my body at his words. "Now get your sexy ass in the car. I'm going to find us a hotel to stop over in. We can drive the rest of the way tomorrow. You've worn me out."

Chapter 28

ghosts

Blake

LOOKING UP AT THE HOUSE that held such a mix of things for both her and me, although mine were only known to me and the guilt of everything that went down here ate away at me especially when I woke up to the apple scent of her shampoo invading my senses; her soft supple body resting completely on mine, mewing sounds purring from her as dreams held her captive. I was completely falling, so fast I couldn't catch my breath, was this how it was all supposed to go, was she my sin and my redemption?

"Okay, I'm ready," she says for the fourth time, yet still doesn't

empathy

make a move to actually get out of the car and walk into her parents' house.

Opening my door, I drum my fingers on the hood, my eyes piercing the house where her brother stands on the porch. I left my firearms at home to stop myself from putting a few bullets in him; not enough to be fatal, just a few to give him unbelievable agony.

The passenger door opens before I reach it, her timid lips creasing into a small smile then a frown. I grasp her hand, trying to pass my strength through our palms to her.

"Who the fuck's this?"

Inhale, exhale, close eyes, count, let her soft stroke down my arm ground me to her. Don't kill him... don't kill him. Smiling down at a tense Melody, I nod for her to go on inside. Her eyes dash between me and her piece of shit brother. I slip an arm around her shoulder, dropping a light kiss to her forehead, whispering against her skin. "It's fine, Puya. Go on in."

She reluctantly pulls from me, entering the house. Her brother turns to follow, coming up short when my hand shoots out to grip his fragile neck. I move swiftly, pulling the door closed with my free hand and smashing his frame against the wood panelling. His hands pushing at my chest don't budge me an inch; he's weak in body as well as mind, the little pissant. Closing in around him, my frame much larger than his, I relish in his fear as tears well in his eyes from my choke hold.

"While we're here, you'll show both of us respect or I'll snap your scrawny fucking neck, you got me?"

He tries to nod but he's restricted. I shove myself back from his body, rolling my head to loosen the tension stiffening my shoulders. "Go show your sister some support. Today is a big day."

He flees inside and I take a minute to loosen my rigid posture before following him.

Melody has stopped in front of the mirror that once reflected the people we once were. The pieces hold a memory of the night, her soul fragmented with it. Now all the tiny shards of glass have been brought back together, creating a mosaic.

"You kept it?" she asks.

"It's an antique. I had it fixed. It looks good, right?"

She brushes her fingers over the cracks. "But it's ruined. It'll never be the same again."

I walk to her, placing my hand on top of hers as she brushes down the grooves.

"Just because something got broken doesn't mean it can't be reassembled into something just as beautiful. It's different now. But it once reflected an image of a girl teetering on the edge of life and death. Now it shows a woman who survived it."

I'm risking myself here, but I know she will never know it was me in here that night, and she also knows I've read the files on what happened. "I know it feels like the darkness pulled you under. Like your gravity abandoned you, letting you slip, but you didn't fall, you didn't drown in evil. You survived, Puya. Look at the woman staring back at you, she's learning to breathe in her new life. She didn't die, she's just adapting to cruel circumstance."

"The police reports tell you all that?" she jokes.

"Your eyes tell me that, Puya." I kiss the sensitive tissue below her ear, making her sigh.

"So, you guys are later than I expected."

I feel her blush without having to see it. "We're here now," she murmurs. "I want to get a few things while I'm here."

"Fine, but dinner will be ready soon." I turn and glare in his direction as she hurries up the stairs. "Make yourself at home."

Like you have, you little fuck. I swallow my retort and make my way into the dining room.

You would never believe chaos ensued here. Everything is in place, no blood, no death but the smell of fear is still potent in the air, or maybe that's just my twisted memories. A harsh death leaves a mark on a property. The walls absorb the evil leaving an echoing memory haunting the place.

I need to call Ryan. I left and didn't even tell him where I was going. He had someone there when I made it back, and by the noises and heavy music thundering through the walls, I didn't want to know what kind of party he had in his room.

Chapter 29

Inheritance

Melody

HE'S SITTING IN HER SEAT. Oh God, the walls are closing in. How can he even use the dining room like it never happened? My mother took her final breath in that chair. She probably had no idea what even happened when she choked on her own blood.

"Mel, come eat." Markus mocked lifting up his spoon. What is that? Red syrup oozes, dripping onto the table. The dripping becomes louder with every beat of my heart, roaring in my ears. Blood everywhere, dripping from the table, creating a river flowing straight towards me. No…no…NO!

"Puya, wake up!"

My body rattles from the force of Blake's arms shaking me. My eyes fly open to rest on his worried face. "You wouldn't wake up. Fuck, you were in a nightmare and I couldn't wake you." His voice trembles, jarring me from my own tremors.

"I'm okay. I'm sorry, I just lay down for a minute. I didn't mean to fall asleep."

"I didn't really let you get much sleep last night. I take full responsibility."

The anxiety fades into comfort. He didn't let me sleep much; he held me and asked me things about myself.

"Favourite Color?"

"Yellow"

"Book?"

"I couldn't possibly narrow it down to one."

"Music?"

"Classical."

"Shit, really?"

"Hmmm, my mom's influence. Country was my dad's, and soft rock is my own."

"Film?"

"Bram Stoker's Dracula."

"Coke or Pepsi?"

That one gave me a chuckle. He was so serious, too. He became like a teenager meeting a girl for the first time. I didn't ask questions about his mom but I knew he had lost his father and Blake became the parent. It's a shit ton of responsibility to have on your shoulders at eighteen. He was headstrong, brave and remarkable for doing it all, putting himself through school and training, and making sure Ryan went to college.

I let him keep asking and answered until he asked me my favourite sexual position. When I shrugged he insisted I find one and I did, reverse cowgirl, he called it. It was me riding him backwards. I feel the heat creeping up my cheeks at the thoughts.

"The lawyer's downstairs. That's why I came up to get you." Blake's voice pops my thoughts like a bubble. My insides twist into the all too familiar ache.

empathy

He coaxes me to my feet and leads me down the stairs.

I close my eyes, praying they haven't convened in the dining room, and sigh when Blake's gentle tug pulls me in the direction of the study.

A grey suit matching grey hair and age-lined features greet me. Mr Dolby had been a friend of my father since I could remember.
"Hello, Melody. I'm so sorry for your loss. As you know, your family have been more than my clients. I favoured your father as one of my friends." I offer him my hand, the grooves in his aging palm swipe across mine, encompassing my much smaller hand in his. "The reading of the will is to be done only in the company of both Melody and Markus. I'm sorry, I didn't get your name." He looks at Blake.
The smirk from Markus is fleeting when he introduces himself as a detective. He actually blanches when the words leave Blake's lips, like a spoken blow lashing across the space and hitting him in the stomach. Even his face has paled. A shiver races up my spine.
"I'll be outside, Mel," he reassures me, closing me in the room with the two men.
I sit through his legal jargon, trying not to snap at Markus for bouncing his knee constantly. He just wants to know what he has coming to him.
"Markus, something recently came to light and I'm sorry to be the one to tell you both this. The fact is, you may not be the biological child of Mr Masters."
All the oxygen in the room evaporates with the pulse of Markus' wrath. His chair flies across the room, his palms crashing down on the table. "That's bullshit!"
Shifting in his seat, Mr Dolby looks over his papers. "This document clearly states your own mother recently divulged this information to Mr and Mrs Masters, to which the will was changed until proof can be provided."
That would explain why I never felt any connection to him.
"That fucking bitch!" I jump from the venom in his tone about his own mother.
"It's a mistake. We can have the tests done, right?" I ask, trying to

tame the building anger pouring from Markus.

"Yes, it's a simple test and the results will be back to you in a week or two."

Pacing the carpet, Markus mumbles about the years he put in, earned him his money.

"Can I have some alone time with Melody for a moment, please?"

Angry blue eyes slash to me before Markus storms from the room slamming the door behind him.

"Melody, your father believed Markus has known this truth for some time now and kept up the pretence to receive his trust fund."

My head swims with the overload of information. I need air and proof before I can do anything else.

"You will become sole heir to your father's fortune, Melody. Your father left you well protected and in capable hands. I can manage your affairs like I have always done for your parents if you wish."

I stand, stroking the creases from my ruffled dress. "I do, thank you. I just need to have the results before we proceed with anything else."

"I understand. The funeral has all been arranged to your mother's specifications. The service will be tomorrow, a small gathering at your mother's church. A joint plot."

I'm going to throw up. My mother had planned her own funeral? How morbid have you got to be to be to plan your death in your forties?

"A responsible parent prepares for all life's possibilities so their loved ones don't have the hard task of dealing with it amongst their grief."

I hadn't realised I spoke aloud, and his reply makes me feel worse for judging her actions when, just like always, she was looking out for me.

Chapter 30

Empathy

Blake

THE SERVICE WAS SMALL AND intimate, but Melody didn't engage with anyone but me. I'm the devil's spawn, I must be. How could I be so callous as to actually attend their funeral? I shook hands, nodded and exchanged greetings with all the people who cared about the deceased. My biggest sin was actually falling for their daughter, but this will get me an extra flaying when I do go to Hell. Fate created this for us though. It had to be, there was no other possibility.

I needed space. I needed to have some semblance of the old Blake to get me through the day. Markus was a time bomb, there was no way in hell I could leave her with him so instead, I went through the motions. Pretending and slipping a smokescreen into place was not something new for me, but I'd never hated myself for it before.

Melody is fucking up everything I perfected over the years. This cold freeze I let take me over was to protect myself, and with her thaw comes the incredible euphoria of her and everything she is, but it also brings guilt, remorse, pain, betrayal, abandonment and regret. It's almost crippling. I need to find a balance between the two.

Melody fell asleep an hour ago; we're approaching her dorm. She didn't argue when I told her we needed to get back today, she was ready to be out of that house and away from the brother she may not have. This is why he hired him. It was all slotting together, Markus knew and wanted rid of the Masters' before they found out and locked him out. But he was too late. Melody's misery. Their bloody murder, all for nothing.

"Oh, I fell asleep."

Looking over to the dishevelled Melody, I reach across to rub a hand down her thigh.

"You were tired. It's been a long couple of days. I brought you back to your dorm."

Looking out the window then back to me, she smiles. "Okay, than..." Her words die on her lips. "Is that Ryan?"

I follow her gaze, and sure enough, Ryan is storming towards us. Cold, dark eyes void of emotion pierce me through the glass. Anger rolls off him in waves.

He yanks Melody's door open, making her flinch back. "You selfish bitch! Where have you been?"

Leaping from my seat, I fly around the car, pointing my finger in his face when he turns his stance on me. "Rein it the fuck in, Ry. What the hell is wrong with you?"

"Don't touch me," he replies with eerie calm. I stare at the kid I raised, searching for him.

"I had to bury my parents, Ryan."

He looks down at her. "You can't use a phone? What have I told you about finding a way to reply to me in future?" He is deadly serious.

Face pinching in confusion and then soothing out, she steps from the car. "Ryan, I don't understand why you're acting like this, but I'm tired."

"Sean died."

Her purse drops from her hand, the contents spilling free onto the sidewalk. "What?"

"They brought him back, but it was touch and go."

I shove his shoulder. "You don't start with 'someone died' unless they stay dead, Ry!"

He ignores me, looking back at Melody. "He walked out in front of a car, right in front of me. It was horrible."

Sean is the blond kid I'm pretty sure has a thing for Ryan. I don't want to see my brother in pain but he seems to be, which explains the anger. I can't fault him on the same thing I'm guilty of; we both turn pain into anger.

"I'm sorry, Ry." Her tiny body wraps him in her embrace, which he accepts and returns, staring at me over her shoulder. "We should go to the hospital."

"I can drive you," I offer.

Twenty minutes later I drop them at the hospital, Ryan making it clear he doesn't want me coming in with them. "Just pick us up in a couple of hours."

I let him give me an order out of respect for him hurting right now which is a whole new side of him. I'm tired anyway and need some space. The last week has been a whirlwind and it's taken its toll, exhausting my mind as well as my body. I'm grateful I had so many holidays stored up that work let me take time off without question.

The unfamiliar black pickup in my driveway has my police training kicking into gear, my mind registering the plate, my eyes assessing the house and surroundings, but time stops when a man jumps from the truck and walks towards me.

I exit my car and stare at him; gun metal eyes with flecks of green, a mirror image of my own unique eye color stands in front of me. "Hello, Damien."

Damien?

"My name's Blake."

The man's brow furrows. Shit, I look so much like him, just a younger version. He has dark hair, age signs tinting the sides with highlights. He's easily six foot three, a strong build, and he looks like he keeps in shape. He doesn't look like the drunken loser my mother always claimed he was.

"Blake, I'm sorry. I sent letters but they went unanswered so I wanted to come here and try in person."

I blanch, hating myself for showing him any weakness, but truth is I have father issues. When you're told by your mom that your dad couldn't flee the town fast enough when he learned about you, and then you got a stepdad who liked to use you as a punch bag, you tend to believe you're a piece of shit no father could want or love. Fuck them both. I don't need anything from them to show my worth. He was a coward for leaving his kid, and the other piece of shit wasn't even worth my thoughts.

"I didn't get any letters, and you're trespassing."

The gentle nod tells me he expected this reaction. "I'm sorry for showing up. I know it's twenty-five years too late."

"Twenty six. My birthday was yesterday."

I haven't celebrated a birthday since my eighteenth, just let them come and go. Yesterday wasn't about me. Melody needed me and I was acting like a whipped choir boy with her. Like I'd gotten my dick wet for the first time. She's the best I've ever had but she clouds me in her beauty and light and it's making me weak.

I actually want to hear his excuse. I want it to be worthy of forgiveness. I want him to tell me he didn't run and leave me with a twisted, hateful bitch but I also want to let my anger feed me into not giving a shit again so it doesn't leave this ache in my stomach. She's making possibilities I didn't think were ever an option for me, there for the taking and as much as I'm feeling, falling without my own permission, part of me doesn't want to open myself up to every emotion that goes with it. I sat through a funeral feeling sick with remorse, I spent the nights with a woman I care about wrapped in my arms and now I'm standing in front of my father, wanting him to see the apple of his eye and not the rotten core inside. I feel six not twenty-six and I hate it all, my mind is a jumbled, screwed up mess. It was easier when I didn't let emotions in. I don't want to love, I don't want to feel, I don't want empathy.

empathy

"This is my address. I don't want to pressure you, but you have siblings who would love to meet you."

Hell, it's like a sucker punch straight in my chest. He hands me a slip of paper. "I didn't know about you, Blake. Until a couple of months ago. I ran into your mom. She was drunk and spilled you out like it was nothing, like she didn't rob me of a son." His voice thickens with emotion.

I can't handle it. I abandon him on the drive, and head into the house. I listen for the roar of his engine and the crackle of the stones under his wheels. I have research to do on him. My mother just keeps coming with her blows. She's poison, infecting and destroying everything she touches.

I ignore the blinking of the answer phone. Six new messages on the house phone. I know it's Abby, she's been blowing up my cell too, but as much as I have all these new emotions swirling around inside me, I still feel nothing for her. Okay, maybe a little shitty for the way I treated her but even that's a lie. I recognise that the way I treated her was shitty. That's good enough, right? Fuck it, I really don't have room to care. I don't even know myself right now and need sleep.

Chapter 31

Healing

Melody

IT'S BEEN TWO WEEKS SINCE I buried my parents. The ache is still there but it isn't as excruciating. Blake is a part of my everyday life. I live and breathe him. He has days when I think what he's feeling will almost suffocate him. I find his eyes on me, the look so intense I feel it right down to my soul. He's affectionate and caring towards me, but our sex is extreme. He unleashes his darker side that lurks in that conflicted part of him. Every day I yearn more for him, I can never see myself tiring of his touch. He has shown me a side of myself I never knew existed, awoke a sexual fiend in me and I love when he brings her out to play. My body is constantly in a state of sexual contentment. The self-defence classes have built my fitness and stamina to rival his and my heart is healing. I'm completely and conclusively in love and it's so powerful it overcomes me, making me clutch at my chest to hold my heart in place so it doesn't beat from my chest.

Ryan is acting peculiar, almost possessive of our friendship, demanding my time away from Blake. Sean is making a full recovery but there is a change in him. He refuses to see me and Blake and is going home to his parents to heal. Blake says it's a normal reaction. He just needs time, so I obey his wishes.

I can't wait for class to let out; I'm almost bouncing in my seat, my pulse thumping heavily with thoughts of Blake. I need him to sate me before he leaves for a two night trip on police business.

"You're vibrating, what the hell's wrong?"

I look at Ryan and bite my lip, embarrassed. "My mind is somewhere else today."

His eyes study mine and then he rolls them. "Is Blake waiting for you?"

I can't help the smile as I nod my head.

"You two need to come up for air every now and then."

I slip my stuff into my bag. "He will be gone for two nights."

"Good. I say house party while he's away, let people know." He doesn't wait for a response, he's out of his seat and trotting down the stairs before I'm even on my feet. Blake will go mad if we have a party while he's away. I feel torn with this kind of stuff because Ry is my friend. I won't invite or tell Blake, that way I'm neutral, I convince myself, rushing from class.

I'm surprised he isn't here to pick me up. He has been the last few days. I make my way to his house instead. I step out of my car and halt as a woman comes flying from his house, her face all flushed. She doesn't acknowledge me as she makes her way to her car. She's left the door ajar.

I hesitantly push it open, the pit opening up in my stomach. I hate walking into the unknown. Anxiety lives in me and I don't think it will ever pass. I breathe deeply and step inside. Hearing movement upstairs, I follow it and find Blake coming out of the room he keeps locked, wearing only his jeans. They are slung low on his hips, his torso all toned and delicious, rippling with the movement of him doing up his belt.

My heart is dying even though that proves nothing and I'm being an irrational woman, I can't help the sick feeling twisting my insides. As if he senses me, his head lifts. His eyes widen then his mouth turns up into a smile. "Hey, I was just coming to get you." He quickly turns, locking the door.

"Who was that woman, Blake?"

He looks down the stairs then back to me. "A girl I fucked."

My legs give out. I crumble to the floor, my heart slowing to almost a stop. Did he really just say that like it's nothing, like it's okay to be fucking someone else? I feel like I'm in a wind tunnel; there's a roaring in my ears.

He's kneels in front of me, laughing. "Puya, I meant used to! God, you could have fallen down the fucking stairs."

Is he seriously laughing at me? "What?"

His face irons out, his eyes softening. "She's kind of an ex, I suppose."

I push his hands away as they reach to stroke a stray tear from my cheek. "You bastard. Why was she here? And what's in that room?"

His eyes lose their heat. "It's my office, I've told you that."

I shake my head, thoughts of the flushed girl fleeing, him being half dressed coming out of a room he keeps locked. Oh my God. "It's a red room, isn't it?"

His brow furrows. "It's painted white."

I stand and he walks to his bedroom with me hot on his tail. "A Christian Grey red room, Blake!"

He grabs a shirt from his dresser, holding it up. "Who is Christian Grey? And, Mel, am I getting dressed or are you going to stop *PMS*ing and get naked?"

I pull my shoe off and throw it at him; he ducks, making it collide with the iPod dock behind him. "You're a fucking crazy bitch." He storms over to me, grabbing me by the hair.

I slap at his chest. "Get off me, you asshole."

He shoves me towards the bed and I land in a heap.

"What's a red room?" he demands, gripping my foot and pulling my other shoe off as I kick at his bare chest, his shirt abandoned.

"A BDSM room." I glare.

He squints then bursts into a loud chuckle holding his stomach. My mouth is agape. He composes himself. "You women and your imaginations. Who is this guy and how the hell do you know him?" His humor is gone, his eyes slaying me.

"He's from a book," I huff. His posture relaxes and he leans forwards, popping the buttons on my jeans. I slap at his hands, making him growl. "Don't touch me, Blake. Why was she here?"

Pulling up and away from me he grabs his shirt from the top of the dresser, putting it on. "She came to ask me about you! She has feelings for me but as you know, I don't feel the same way."

I sit up, doing up the buttons on my jeans.

His eyes narrow "I can't be dealing with this jealous bullshit, Melody. If I wanted to be fucking her, I would be, but I'm not. You're the only one I want and that's new for me."

I stalk towards him. "Well, let's give you a prize for not being a slut and cheating on me like you clearly did her."

He grabs my arm, stopping my retreat. "I didn't cheat on her because I've never had a woman who was mine before you!"

I need him to tell me what we are. I need to know he feels this as deeply as I do. "Am I yours, Blake?"

Grasping my cheeks he brings his lips down to my mouth, whispering across them. "I know if any other man touches you, I'll kill him. I know that I never want to be inside another woman when I have your perfection to sink into." *Well that's kind of romantic; he just needs to work on his wording.* "Don't let insecurities infest your mind, Mel. It's not an attractive quality and I have low tolerance for this woman shit."

And there he goes and ruins it. "I hate you," I murmur, feeling defeated.

"No you don't, you love me and that's why you're acting crazy." He lifts me, throwing me on the bed for second time. "I'm going to fuck that crazy shit right out of you."

And he does and leaves me sated and naked in his bed.

I wake, groaning from the pleasant ache between my thighs. He left his mark in the form of love bites painting my skin in red and purple blotches up my inner thighs, across my breasts and stomach and his favourite place to leave them - my mound. That was his goodbye before leaving me.

His heavy breaths on top of me is a sound I want to record and listen to over and over. I pull the covers further up my body and jump when I see Ryan staring at me.

"Ryan, I'm naked. What are you doing in here?" He seems to be in a trance. I look at the open door and then at him; he's holding an object in his hand, his fist grasping it so tight his knuckles are white. I sit up and slowly scoot towards him. It's a corkscrew.

"Ryan," I whisper. His hand shoots forwards, startling me again, the pointed end of the corkscrew mere centimetres from my eye.

"I opened you some wine. Come down and drink it."

My breathing is non-existent. His hand drops and he stalks off. What the actual hell?

I rush to get dressed, noticing it's two a.m. Music is playing and when I turn into the living room there's a girl dancing on the coffee table. She's wearing a short leather skirt and a thin piece of fabric over her chest. When I get closer I see something wrapped around her head; it's a ball gag, her mouth holding the ball. She seems to not mind.

"Here, drink up. I called you a cab."

I pick my jaw off the floor and shake my head to his offering of wine. "You could have left me sleeping, Ry."

He looks at the girl and then at me. "I can't risk having you here when I'm like this," he mumbles.

Heels click across the floor and a woman in full leathers struts into the room towards us. My eyes nearly fall from my head and I turn to Ryan.

"I need you to leave for the night. We can hang tomorrow."

empathy

"Unless she wants to stay and play?" The woman smirks. She bends forward to an open bag and brings out another gag.

I march from the house as a cab pulls up. I give the driver a twenty and tell him I have my car.

I miss him. I missed him before he even left, which is crazy but I'm crazy in love and it wreaks havoc with my emotions. I just want to crawl inside him and live there. I want to constantly hear his heartbeat so I know he's here, living and breathing. I'm one of those annoying women who live for their man. Urgh, I'm pathetic. I check my phone, there's nothing from him, and no reply to my texts asking if he made it safely.

Ryan has left me a voicemail telling me to pick things up for the party tonight and to get round there to help set up. I'm still not comfortable with it but the longer I don't hear from Blake, the more I needed the distraction.

The house is bustling with people, and music resonates through the walls giving the house a pulse. How he managed to get so many people to turn up on such short notice was surprising and unfortunate. The clean-up is going to be messy and Blake is going to kick our asses.

My phone vibrates against my chest from where I stored it in my bra. I don't trust to just leave it somewhere. I hardly recognise anyone except Red and Cherry who are practically vibrating with excitement, both wanting to catch Ryan's eye. I've never revisited the time he made that woman choke giving him head. I don't know if those girls could handle him but it isn't my place to talk about his business so I guess if they're willing to make a play they'll either have to enjoy the ride or leave the park he likes to play in.

Blake's name flashes on my screen and my unsettled nerves from not hearing from him fizzle when I accept the call and hear his voice. "Hey."

I rush outside to get away from the noise, but I'm not quick enough. "Tell me that's not a party at my house, Melody?"

I swallow. He hardly ever uses my given name. "Ryan invited some people over." The rowdy noises in the background light up my lie.

"I can't believe this. Very mature, Mel. Shit, you should be dating him." That hurts.

"Nice, Blake. I haven't heard from you and this is what you want to say to me?"

Crackles down the line from his exhale make me pull the phone away slightly. "I can't deal with this. Call me when you stop the needy woman shit."

The phone goes dead and so does my heart. The few drinks I had earlier magnify my emotions.

Stepping back inside, I come to a halt. The girl I saw fleeing here is staring at me. Screw this; I can be the bigger person.

"Hey, I'm Melody. I saw you leaving here yesterday."

"Yes, you did. He will chew you up too. He's incapable of love." She's hurting so I just nod my head, she doesn't need me telling her that he just couldn't love her. "He will never commit or give up his trips and privacy. Have you ever seen inside the office he keeps locked?"

"Have you?"

She narrows her eyes. "No, no-one has, that's the point. He has secrets, and from the way he is emotionally deficient, they can't be good secrets." She brushes past me as she leaves. I hate that she's making me paranoid but I can't lie to myself. I don't understand why he is the way he is. What can he have in his office that has to be kept such guard of?

I look around at the people all laughing, dancing and filling the downstairs of the house to capacity. I stalk to the kitchen, rummaging through the drawers and find a screwdriver.

I march up the stairs, and a guy comes from the bathroom and

empathy

smiles at me. "Hey."

I wave and he stops, his eyes raking over me. Shit, does everyone think saying *hey* at a party is a come on?

"Hey back." He lifts his chin, trying to be sexy and I hold back my cringe.

I need him. I hold up the screwdriver and his eyes widen, questioning me.

"Can you help me out? I need to get into my room. I locked it to keep party goers out but then lost the key." I pout.

He grins. "Sure thing." He makes quick work of unscrewing the door from its frame. Ha, that was pretty easy, maybe it's not kept under heavy guard. Ignoring a few questioning looks from people going to use the bathroom. I feel like a crazy girlfriend now but I let the alcohol give me false courage.

The guy looks inside, his brow furrowing. "Where's your bed?"

I step inside. The white walls are bare, there's nothing but a safe and a computer desk with a laptop on.

"I sleep on the floor, I get back pain," I tell him. He shrugs and leaves.

I pace the small empty space, wringing my hands together before building the courage to go over to the desk. It has three drawers down the front on the right hand side, leaving a gap for the office chair to the left. Opening the laptop, the screen powers up and prompts me for a password. I drum my fingers on the desk, debating whether to try guessing but I know it will be impossible and may alert Blake to the fact someone tried and failed. Instead I try the drawers and pull one open, surprised it isn't locked. There is a bundle of papers in there, some with addresses on. I lift out the contents and sift through, ignoring the gnawing guilt in my stomach. The feeling is fleeting and soon turns into a nervous sickness.

I fall back into the seat when I see me. My life, my family. I examine paper after paper, all filled with information on me. My aunt, half-brother; my father's wealth and business. The room is closing in around me, the air being sucked out. All noise from the people downstairs fades. Everything stills including my heartbeat when I come to documents dated back to when my parents were killed.

Why would Blake have all this? How long has he been investigating their murder? Sucking at the air to fill my lungs I close my eyes and count slowly to ten. Timidly opening them again, I read the document clutched in my fist.

> Mr and Mrs Masters
> Clean Kill Fee paid $300,000
> Complications charges if they arise $50,000

A hot pulse of despair races through my system. Someone paid $300k to kill the people I would pay everything I own and more to have back? Why didn't the killer go to my father and ask for more in exchange for his life? Tears blur my vison, soaking my cheeks. I swipe angrily at them. The police haven't told me any of this information, they just spun me lies. *Unless Blake hasn't shared his findings yet.* I turn over the next page, my breath seizing.

> Ordered hit by Markus Masters (son).

No. No!

I can't breathe. I look around but there's no window. I rush from the room, down the stairs and out of the house, retching. I lose the drink I consumed to the flower bed. Markus hired someone to kill our dad? Oh my God. He's still being awkward about getting the paternity test done so I still don't know if he was our Dad or just mine. Markus stole him, stole both of my parents from me.

Blake is investigating my parents' murder. Is that why he's with me? I'm drowning from my own heart bursting. I can't understand this. I walk back through the door and grab a bottle of Jack Daniel's then head back out and jump into my car. I need to be alone.

Chapter 32

Heart

Blake

I CAME TO WATCH MY father with his family. I have two sisters. It's weird, always living life just for Ryan and then tumbling down the rabbit hole straight into love with Melody, and now I'm looking at miniature versions of myself in female form, and God willing, not harboring the internal battle with a beast. I was tormented when I called Melody and upset her. Her voice always wavers when she's upset. I need to have words with Ryan, this shit is getting old fast, but first I need to go to her. I phone to tell her I'm coming back early. I'm only an hour out.

I track her GPS in her phone which leads me to her dorm and I use the key I copied from hers.

She sways her hips slowly, her lips mouthing the lyrics to a soft rock ballad playing from her iPod. She's feeling the beat, moving in sync with it. Tears leaks from her eyes when they clash with mine, emotions heightened from the bottle of Jack, half full on the table.

I creep from the shadows, stalking towards her, the tint from the moonlight highlighting her. Her tattoo is right. She blossoms in the dark because I am the darkness and with me she blossoms. When we're apart we're just shadows, apparitions of souls that used to be there. We never really had much, and what we had was taken from us, but we found each other. She was sent to thaw me, to bring back my warmth.

I slip a hand around her waist, my body encompassing hers. I bury my face in her hair and inhale her, the apple shampoo she uses washes over me with familiarity and my heart thuds against my chest. My fingertips skim the hem of her top, she doesn't need directions, her arms lift for me to skim the material from her. Dropping it to the floor I stroke back, down her arms and across her chest that's lifting with her desperate pants mixed with sobs. She's still raw from our argument.

"Why did you want me?" she whispers.

It's a question most women want to know. *Why them* and among the deceit I keep from her out of necessity I don't want to lie to her.

Skimming my hand down her torso, her body shuddering under my touch, I push her shorts and panties down her hips, my fingertips never leaving her skin. I lower myself down with them so I can lift her foot, freeing her completely so I can bask in her nakedness. God, she's beautiful. On my knees, looking up at her, I wrap my arms around her hips, my hands grasping her ass and bringing her forward so my face can seek out the scent of her arousal. I breathe her in and relish in her whimper. She smells of heaven. I pull back my eyes showing her the intensity of how much I need her.

"I didn't want you." She flinches, her hands coming down to push against my shoulders. "I never wanted anyone. I lived my life detached, cold and then one day you crashed into me, dislodging something inside me. You refused to leave me, like fate placed you there for the sole purpose of making me realise I'm still human, that I don't have to live in the darkness of the past."

Her eyelids flutter as more tears cascade from her eyes. Standing, I stroke the pads of my thumbs across her reddened cheeks and bring my lips down to kiss her now closed eyes. I lift her onto the bed and savor the gentle, delicate moment between us. I breathe heavy, finding the words I feel and she deserves to hear. "I love you. God, I love you. I didn't think I could ever love anyone but it's here." I grasp her hand and place it over my heart. "You make this beat harder, I feel you here, I feel your soul, it's wrapped around mine, cleansing me, inundating me with so much love I feel like I may crumble under the weight of it. I never knew I could feel this and now I do it's so intense I'm scared of it, scared to fuck it up. It grows with every second that passes. I love you."

Worshipping her body, every inch of warm flesh, kissing each fingertip, her palms, up her delicate wrists, down her arms raising them above her head and skimming my lips down the side of her chest. Her skin tastes like candy from the lotions she smothers herself in. I'm completely drunk on the scent, the taste. Her body shivers under my attention, she's used to our rushed, raw passion but I need to relish in the flavor of her beauty.

Her pants echo through the room, adding to the soft beats coming from her music. I trace a path across her navel, licking out to taste her. I go lower, making her pant harder, her little whimpers make me anxious to be inside her. I move down to show her pretty pussy the same tender kisses I've shown the rest of her body. She's on fire, her arousal igniting my primal need to be rough and dive into her. I need to taste the wet heat beneath me. I swipe my tongue between her folds, groaning as her taste sparks my taste buds, circling her throbbing clit, her moans making me fucking crazy. Her hips lift to my mouth, begging. I continue to tease, bringing her to the brink but not giving her what she needs.

"Blake!" It's a plea whispered on the thick, hunger-filled air. I bring two fingers to join my mouth, delving into her hot depths, her tight walls squeezing them. Her body is writhing, she's slipped into a state of intoxicated desire and it's gorgeous. "More, Blake!"

"More what? What do you need, Puya? Tell me?"

"Harder!"

I suck on her clit and pound my fingers into her. She comes undone under my tongue, her pussy pulsing around my fingers. I lift my head to watch the final throes wash through her. She reaches down and grabs my wrist, moving it up and down as my fingers continue to work her pussy, it's sexy as fuck having her guide the rhythm of my hand, her hips rising to gain friction against her clit. A mist of sweat coats her skin making her glow under the moonlight.

I can't hold back any longer. I pull free from her, making her groan, mourning the loss. I grip her hips and indicate for her to turn over; she complies turning onto her stomach, lifting her ass up to me, offering me what I need.

Stripping my clothes off I crawl over her body, kissing her shoulders and down her spine. My hands follow the same path. I lick the dimples at her lower back and sink my teeth into her ass cheek. She whimpers then moans when I lick the sting away. I raise her hips further and sink straight into her, her pussy grips me. I lean forward, bringing my hand underneath her, my other hand in her hair gripping tight and tugging her head back so I can get access to her perfect tits. I buck my hips into her and she matches me thrust for thrust, her body rocking against mine, skin on skin, my front covering her entire back, my elbow the only thing keeping my weight from crushing her into the mattress. Tugging more firmly on her hair, I bring our bodies to the side so her front is completely accessible to my hand. My lips latch on to hers as I piston into her, my other hand slipping between her legs. Pinching and tapping her clit with gentle slaps have her moaning, playing a chorus to the beat of the music. Her hand lies on top of mine as she guides us together to rub her clit. Her pussy convulses, strangling my cock and she calls out my name. I bite down on her shoulder and thrust a few more times before succumbing to the pleasure her body gives me.

Our heavy breaths are the only sound now. I reach for her duvet and pull it over us, keeping her pinned against me. She doesn't fight, and within minutes her breathing evens out and I follow her into sleep.

Chapter 33

Preparing

Melody

I'M IN A FURNACE, SWEAT coating mine and Blake's skin, moulding us together. Damn, my head hurts., the bottle of Jack playing its encore through my body. My stomach vaulting. I shove at Blake's heavy frame and he grumbles, turning over onto his back completely naked, his morning glory on full salute. No matter how rough or fragile I feel, just seeing him proud and ready makes me dampen between my thighs. I need to relieve my bladder and drink water. Lots and lots of water.

"Come back to bed." The vibrating echo of Blake's voice follows me to the bathroom.

"Shower." I call back.

Two hours later we pull up to the aftermath of the party. I swallow the nerves of him finding his office door off its hinges. I text Markus to tell him I need to come home to talk to him; he replies *tomorrow*. Fine, tomorrow it is. That gives me time to let my anger fester, let the fuel of my grief rise. I will not hold my tongue, I will not show mercy when I throw everything I have at him. I'm ready to explode and I want it all aimed at him.

"You coming in?"

"Yeah. I can't stay long. I need to go to class and I have my self-defence class tonight."

"It's fine, Mel. I have work tonight too."

The house is spotless. My jaw unhinges and Blake's fingers caress my cheek. "He's a clean freak, Mel. There's never a mess when I come home, just sluts lurking, usually."

Shit. You would never know that just hours before, the house was at full capacity with students.

I follow him upstairs, my eyes bulging at the closed, locked office door. Oh my God, I love Ryan in this moment; he saved my ass. I jump when Blake's foot collides with Ryan's bedroom door, forcing it to fly open and ricochet off the wall behind it.

"Get the fuck up and get to class with Melody, now. I'm getting really sick of your shit. Every time I leave you, you act out like some kid!"

With that he waltzes out and over to me, crushing his lips to mine. "I'll call you tonight when I get off work, okay?"

Class drags. I need to rethink my courses. I'm not enjoying college at all. I'm thinking about investing some money into a small newspaper business that's struggling in my home town against its much bigger rival. I'm young and still need an education behind me but it's a huge step in the direction I want to take my career. The prospect of going into business would never have crossed my mind at this age before my tragic loss. It forced many changes in my life. I'm growing up at lightning speed. I want to make my parents proud of me. I won't die

empathy

from my wounds I will own them and fight life right back.

"Kick, punch," My instructor shouted at me. I paid for private classes so if I did freak out he would be the only one to witness it. I had enough crap flying around thanks to that woman Abby. Sweat beaded against my forehead, my whole body was soaking. He worked me hard and I was grateful I needed to know how to protect myself, especially with my plans to confront Markus. "Brilliant Melody, you're doing amazing. Go shower."

I gulped at the water his pregnant wife handed me coming into the studio. She was stunning five months pregnant and glowing. "Thank you Colleen," I breathed and returned her bright smile.

The hot water eased my muscles. I made quick work of it drying off and throwing on some clean sweats. Blake had text to say he was coming to pick me up and spend the night. I would have to sneak out in the morning before he wakes.

Chapter 34

Dark urges

Ryan

CLIVE CATCHES MY EYE AS I pump gas into my truck. He's with Jacob, trying to chat up the attendant who seems more interested in the celeb mag she's leaning into, diverting her eyes from the two morons. I'm off to Club Nine tonight and this run in will be an inconvenience. I would usually appreciate bumping into Clive and letting him go a few rounds with his fists but the part of my brain that hates to lose tells me I've already let him get away with too much.

A shiver races through my body with the possibilities of what tonight could bring. The thing about most people who harbor a beast inside them, including Blake, is they believe they lack emotions yet they fight the sinister pull in themselves. They quash urges, conform to what society expects from them. They bury the wicked fiend, but not me, I'm friends with mine. I like his rule. I obey his commands and indulge in the sickness.

I'm not delusional. I know there is something missing in me. I was born missing the defining element that makes us human but I was still born and therefore must live with who I am… what I am. I am the beast. Blake let his soul slip into obscurity but mine was never there to begin with and there is nothing inside that tells me I shouldn't be what I was created to be.

"What are you staring at?" Clive spits at me.

I was so engrossed in my depraved thoughts I didn't see him come out of the store. I wiggle the trigger to the gas pump and put it back into place.

Turning to face him, I shrug my shoulders. "Nothing, I was lost in thoughts of getting laid."

He squints at me, his upper lip curling. "Like you can get laid, freak."

God he is such a cliché, it's almost too easy. "Club Nine has the best pussy there is and I love sampling all they have to offer."

His face morphs into disbelief. "That's a fetish club. I knew you were a freak."

I roll my eyes. "It's pussy on tab. If liking to get my dick wet by the best lays makes me a freak, then you're right, I'm a freak." I smirk for effect.

"How the fuck do you get in there? It's a private club from what I hear."

Little shit has looked into it. I know he's not a virgin, I can sense that on someone. I'm a good judge of character but I'm betting he has never been with anyone who knows what they're doing. I won't tell him I let the owner live out his fantasies on me which gets me anything I want from the club; this is something Blake is unaware of too or another soul would be added to his death toll. Although the owner is male and likes to fuck me up the ass while I pretend to cry, the twisted fuck, I'm not gay, I'm just unconcerned about his perversion and bask in having power to hold over him. I watch the picture of his loving family as he lives out his sin, and ponder just how many others were born wrong like me.

"I have a membership and can take guests if I please."

I watch the implication register in Clive's eyes. He flits his eyes to Jacob then back to me, shuffling on his feet. "I don't believe you."

My inner voice wants to berate him for being so pathetic but he's playing into my hands perfectly. "Come with me then."

A quick whisper in Monica's ear telling her I need her for the rest of the night and on top slut form has her winking and clearing any scheduled clients she has. Clive's jaw is agape and we're only in the entry.

"Oh my God, that's my dad," he stutters.

My eyes trace the path to the man he's glaring at, and true to his word, his dad is on the monitor from the main room with some sub at his feet. I've seen him here before but it's forbidden to talk about who has membership here, and the fact he doesn't want me to talk stops him from questioning me being allowed to play here.

"Mmm, so it is."

Monica smirks before slipping into seductress mode, her cleavage, contained by a corset, rubs against Clive's chest when she leans into him and murmurs, "I want you to play with my pussy."

His eyes snap to hers and a grin lightens his features. "Maybe we should take this back to my place? Blake's away for the night," I say.

Within an hour we're all back at my house. Monica brought Trey and Layla with her at my request. Jacob is nervous and tries to bail on us but Clive calls him a pussy and insists he's losing his v-card tonight. Ha, he's right but not in the way Clive suspects. Monica wastes no time stripping naked for Clive's viewing pleasure. I'm surprised he doesn't lose his load before even getting inside her. Her legs spread revealing a well primped cunt.

Layla sidles up to Clive. "Don't just stare at it… eat it," she com-

empathy

mands.

His arousal shows in his glossed over eyes, the flush blazing in his cheeks and the hard on trying to escape his slacks. He looks at me for direction. I lift both eyebrows in a quick motion, making him grin and drop to his knees. He leans straight in, tasting what she offers; her moans and pelvic thrust are a performance she has mastered.

Jacob looks like he's about to lose his stomach over my carpet which will make Blake bitch. I nod to Trey who works his charm on Jacob. By the time Clive has freed his cock and slips into Monica, Jacob has given in to who he is and has Trey taking his virginity over the coffee table. The smell of sex and depravity seeps into the air, feeding my lungs.

When Clive registers the act of Trey ramming his giant cock into little Jacob's ass, his face contorts in confusion and then distaste, making Jacob push Trey away. Jacob stumbles into his clothes and flees.

Layla gains Clive's attention when she begins to suck on Monica's nipples. I need to nourish my own urges, making Jacob break and showing who he is to his best friend put me on a path that needs to be fully played out. I walk up to Layla, gripping her hair in a closed fist and wrenching her from Monica's fake tit. "Upstairs, everyone. I don't want fluids on the couch."

Chapter 35

Consequences

Ryan

I ANSWER THE ANNOYING RINGING. "What?" I bark.

I hear a sniffle down the line and then Melody's croaky voice. "I need you to come somewhere with me. To my home." The sniffles continue.

Fuck, why did I have to make friends with people? When that happens they expect you to be human when they need you.

"Mel, that's a long way. What do you need to go there for?"

I hear her moving around and I sit up, my eyes taking in the sight of last night's action. Shit, I lost it. I knew I would, it had been building.

"I need someone there when I speak to my half-brother."

Interesting.

The consequences of last-night are impossible to hide from. "Fine. Come pick me up."

I step over Clive and shut my door behind me, heading to the shower and rinsing the sin from my body. I've lost it, there's no hiding my perversions anymore.

I dress, and leave when I hear Melody toot the car horn. I slide into the car and look over her face; she's troubled, her eyes glassy. "What's this about, Mel?"

She shakes her head. "I just need to see him. You look wrecked. You can sleep if you want."

I recline the chair and do just that.

I wake with a jolt when the car door slams shut, the lights from the gas station Melody has stopped at makes my head hurt. "I got you a coffee."

I scrub my hands down my face. "How long have we been on the road?" I reach for the cup and wince when the hot liquid burns my tongue. "You can't call that coffee!"

She shrugs. "You've been out four hours."

I must have needed the sleep. I wonder if Blake's home yet. I check my phone to find many missed calls and texts from him. He must have been home. Silencing my phone I slip it into my pocket "You want me to drive for a bit?"

The gravel kicks up as I pull up to her house. I feel her eyes on me. She's expecting me to comment on her house.

"Wow, big."

"Momma didn't think so," she murmurs.

I stretch when I get out and go to the trunk to collect her bag.

"What are you doing? I didn't bring anything, we're not staying."

I cross my arms over my chest. "Mel, we just drove nearly eight hours. I'm not driving back tonight."

She pulls her phone out, staring at the screen. "We can get a hotel then but I can't stay here."

I watch her for a few seconds then concede. Doesn't matter anyway, neither one of us will be getting sleep tonight.

She sighs in relief and slowly, too slowly, climbs the steps. She's shaking. God, she's so weak. It's a house. I take the keys from her hand and open the door, the lights highlight the lobby and I coax her inside by stepping in first.

"Mel, is that you?" her brother calls out, coming to a stop when he sees she's not alone. "Ryan!"

"I'm the boyfriend's brother."

His mouth is agape, his posture rigid. "Well, come in. Go through to the dining room. I'll get drinks."

I turn to Melody. She stares at me, waiting for answers. "We play in some of the same scenes" her features pinch "How is that even possible? Did you know he was my Half-brother, you don't seem surprised at all?" I unclench my jaw her questions are irrelevant at this point in the game "Come on, Mel. There's going to be a lot of revelations today."

I leave her still confused but she follows behind me without further questions.

My phone is going crazy but I ignore it. Everything that had happened had led us here and although it wasn't how I saw it playing out, I didn't expect my brother to regain his humanity and fall for Melody. What are the chances?

Chapter 36

Unseen truths

Melody

THEY KNOW EACH OTHER? HOW small the world is. I hate the complete disregard for my feelings when Markus tells us to go through to the dining room. I don't know why it surprises me. This guy is the soulless coward responsible for my parents' deaths.

Ryan casually sits at the table, drumming his fingers against the dark wood surface. I pace the floor, trying to block out the ghosts that haunt my memories of this room.

"So?" Markus asks, dropping a bottle of whiskey on the table with three tumblers. He must have a sixth sense of what's coming.

Reaching into my jeans pocket I pull out the bundle of paper, scanning through them frantically for the right one. My heart is pounding so loud against my chest I'm worried it will crack the bone. Throwing the paper down on the table, it floats across the polished wood, stopping near the bottle. Ryan looks over, rising slightly to get a better look.

"Where did you get this?" Markus asks. His eyes flick to Ryan. "You fucking sold me out?"

My insides congeal. Did I hear that right? My world tilts on its axle as I look over to my friend.

"Well, this is awkward." Ryan, my friend, Blake's brother, speaks into the room but he sounds far away.

I pull out a chair and quickly drop into it so I don't fall to the floor.

"I got that from his brother. He's a detective, Markus. He was clearly investigating you for murdering my parents. You son of a bitch!"

He doesn't even flinch or try to deny it. He pours a shot of whiskey and pushes the glass towards me. Is he serious right now? I grab the glass and lunge at him, but his arm comes up to protect his face, the glass rebounding from his arm.

"You fucking crazy bitch."

"You're calling me crazy? I will end you for this. When he arrests you I will use every cent you wanted to inherit to make sure you never see the outside of a prison again."

His sneer is deadly, but screw him, I want justice for his greed.

"This," he holds up the piece of paper, "is a contract with the killer, Mel, you fucking idiot!"

Ryan flexes his shoulders.

"You're a contract killer?" I want to laugh at myself for asking but my life is full on crazy right now and I need to voice everything and have it answered so there's no more confusion, no more lies.

"Not me, Mel. Blake."

His words pull the breath straight out of me, and with it, my soul. I'm dying all over again. The fist is tighter than before. It's a lie... it can't be.

"When I first saw you I knew you were special. You provoked me, Melody." Ryan rose from his chair. "Your looks, the brush of your legs against mine. You wanted my attention so you got it. It was fate! I met your brother in Club Nine. He likes a whore there called Vicki, she's a filthy little slut and she looks just like you."

I want to take a rain check on this pain. I can't deal with it anymore. My heart pounds at my chest. Markus is staring at me, wringing his hands together.

"You see, your brother isn't your brother at all and he likes to punish poor little Vicki and pretend it's you. I couldn't believe it when Vicki divulged his kink to me. He calls her Melody while he fucks and disciplines her." Ryan's chuckle is cold; it's weird hearing a laugh from him. I realise I've never really heard him laugh before. "I thought it must be a coincidence but the only reason I was in there fucking Vicki was for the exact same reasons. Because she looks like you. So I made contact, and sure enough, the little pissant was a little on the crazy side, not that I can talk." He pulls a weird face using his finger to swirl at his skull to indicate insanity. "It was fate. I was being tested and served you on a plate! And you made it all so easy, Melody. When Blake's life changed. Death impacted him and completely transformed him but we had an unhealthy upbringing. You, on the other hand, had a perfect set of parents. You shone real bright and I wanted to watch you unravel. I wanted to see how much darkness it would take to dim that light." Pain washes through me, is he playing with my head? His heart was black, rotten and mine was decomposing with every new secret he divulged. "Markus was easy to manipulate."

"Fuck you, Ryan," Markus spits.

The room temperature drops, the air almost alive with an electric current. Ryan moves like a cat striking at prey, his hand grips at Markus' throat. He pulls him against his body and away, then against him again before guiding a stunned Markus into the seat my mother died in. The color drains from his face and he looks down to his stomach, my eyes following in slow motion. Red ink expands across the fabric. Oh no…no…no. This isn't happening.

"Don't look so mortified, Mel. He deserved it. Didn't you want him to pay? And he interrupted my story."

Screams fill the room. Mine. A heaving thud lands against the side of my head, stealing my consciousness.

Chapter 37

Signs

Blake

SHUT THAT OFF, MEL. TURN it off. My eyes adjust to the light streaming in the room, heating it like an oven. Shit it's hot. I'm alone with a note scribbled on a piece of ripped paper on her pillow.

empathy

> *Have to do something. You should have told me.*

What the fuck does that mean? Grabbing my cell - that was what woke me up - I frown at the eighteen missed calls from my partner, Zach. Something must have gone down last night. There's a nervous energy in the air that I can't quite put my finger on. Hitting call back, I wait.

"Blake, thank fuck. I need you to come in. Don't talk to anyone, come straight to evidence room three."

The call disconnects and my mind spins. There's no way they could have anything on me, I'm too careful. Melody's note stares up at me. I try her number and get the answer machine. "Call me straight away when you get this."

Twenty five minutes later I walk with my head down to evidence room three.

Zach rushes over to me, scanning the corridor before closing the door. His hand rubs through his sandy hair.

"What the hell, Zach?"

"Sit down." I don't like taking orders from people but the unease in his voice makes me sit. "New evidence came in about that Club Blue murder. A video from a shop a few blocks up."

"And what took so long?"

He sits in front of me shaking his head. "They were going through footage to find a graffiti tag on their back wall. Anyway, Blake, you need to see this."

He's freaking me out. He turns to the set up and clicks play. The screen comes to life. A dark alleyway sits static on the screen. Moments pass before a figure approaches; it's the suspect. He lifts his blood drenched hoodie over his head and drops it in a trash can. His face comes into full view making me jolt upright, my chair crashing to the floor.

I've done all the courses, felt it in my bones, but ignored it all. I knew in my heart something was wrong with him. Oh God, nearly every person who is close to, related to or a victim of a psychopath utters those words. Did I force him to this? I feel sick. I've killed but never took pleasure in it like he does. I'm not brutal and without cause. I don't kill randomly for fun.

"Blake?" I snap from the haze. "I haven't showed this to anybody else. It came to my desk."

"I need to leave. I need to go to him."

I run from the precinct, driving in a fog of everything in my life playing out up to now. How could I let him become this? How can I save him now?

I try his cell numerous times, getting voice mail. Rushing from the car across our drive I drop the keys trying to open the door, the tremor in my hand a new thing for me.

The house is quiet, the same unsettling atmosphere surrounding me as when I woke up.

"Ryan!"

Taking the stairs two at a time I run along the hall and I bash at his closed door, the hinges rattling from the impact. The door slowly glides open. The roar of my own heartbeat pounds into my skull. Blood. So much blood. This is really happening. I'm breaking apart, falling into the pits of hell. My time has come and this is hell, it has to be.

Fuck, that's Clive. The naked body of the kid from college, eyes open, throat cut. Two women carved up with a blade decorate his bed. God, I can't even determine the death blow, they're riddled with fucking slashes. Blood covers every naked inch of them, the white room painted with their life.

empathy

I pull the door closed, walking down the stairs into the front room. His PC is booted up, a paused video on the screen. I press play, losing my footing, my knee hitting the floor with a thud. Melody lay in his bed wearing the tank and panties I saw her in that first night she stayed here. She lay there motionless as he stood above her, stroking himself. I want to die so I don't have to witness this. He found his release, jumping from the bed to pull out a sweatshirt to wipe her clean with before shoving it back in his bag.

What the fuck? Melody. Where the fuck is she? Where's Ryan?

I boot up my tracking to her GPS. She's on the road. Where the hell is she going?

Chapter 38

Evil

Melody

PRESSURE PUSHES AGAINST MY WINDPIPE. A burn from a freezing sensation stings the soles of my feet, arms keeping me steady release me, the pressure at my throat intensifies. My hands are bound behind my back.

My senses all hit at once and Ryan fills my vision. I'm hanging from the ceiling by a rope around my neck, my feet slipping on ice in a bucket.

"Finally." I can't answer him. I can't scream. "You like the ice? I just thought of it while you were taking a cat nap. If Blake gets here before the ice melts I'll let him cut you down."

He's insane. How had I been so blind to him? The callousness towards others. The disregard for everyone. The sense of superiority. He's possessive and cold but I rationalized it and now the toxic relationship I'd encouraged is destroying me like a disease.

"Blake killed for what he thought was my honour. My father had a thing for young men." I don't want to hear any more. The rope isn't killing me quickly enough. "I used to watch him watch Blake. I knew he was fighting his urges and he did fight them by using violence. Only on Blake, though. All my bruises were self-inflicted to make Blake think he was harming me. That night, the night Blake killed him, I was taunting him. He was jerking it in his room. He chased me into my room and hit me, shouting at me about not being all there in the head." His grin is the strangest thing I've ever seen. "I fell onto the bed and he came over me to throttle me. Blake came in and he let the scene speak for itself. I added some muffled screams for show." He shrugged, like an eleven-year-old orchestrating something so drenched in malice is normal.

A whimper leaves my constricted voice box when I see Blake standing there, soaking in the scene.

"Oh, brother. Just in time for the good bit." Ryan appears in my eye line, blocking me from Blake's view. "He became a killer that night, but he didn't stop. He didn't think I knew he kills for money. So when I came across your…" he lifts his hands to air quote, "brother, planting the idea of hiring someone to kill your folks, he ate it up. I gave him Blake's contact info and boom. Done."

I can't breathe. He's lying. My entire life freezes as cold as the ice beneath my feet. He is lying, right? Oh God. The air in my lungs ceases completely, my world once again tilting on the edge of shattering. My sight blurs as the tightening of the rope depletes me of oxygen.

"It was perfect. I even drove him to the airport and text you while you drove home to meet him."

Every word he spews cuts into me, embedding their truth into my soul, adding more scars to the already wounded essence that's slowly dying.

Chapter 39

Delusions

Blake

SHE'S HANGING FROM THE CEILING, a rope around her neck. Her hands are bound and her legs struggle to keep balance in a bucket filled with ice. He's so far gone I know I'll never find him. I'm so lost in my own skin, I'm not sure if I'll ever find me again. My heart is bleeding with fear for Melody and conflicting choices for Ryan. Hearing him say he set that scene with my step dad. He's been playing me from childhood.

"Whenever I found a bruise on you, I blamed myself for having to go to school or for getting out of that house and being with my friends so I could breathe. Every mark on you, every tear you shed when you showed me, I shared them. God, you killed me slowly, piece by piece. Every night of my life I prayed for the strength to protect you but it cost me. Hell answered the call, my soul was the penance and I vanished little by little, fading into the drag of his corrupted lure, dissolving me of humanity until Melody woke the good in me. The boy who gave up his life for the love of his brother was betrayed by that same brother. It's painful."

His almost black eyes are like looking down the barrel of a gun.

"I know you want me to care, Blake. For you, probably only you, sometimes I wish I could but I just don't. I'm a void. I crave destruction. It's the only thing that gives me any type of feeling."

"Why play with my life so ruthlessly?"

He shrugs. "Because I like the power. Humanity is weak. Love is a weakness, Blake, it was yours. You played at embracing the beast but it was never really yours. You're only the monster I made you."

Melody is losing consciousness; I need to get her down. He knows what I'm thinking; he can read people better than I can. "Cut her down."

I reach for the blade I keep in my boot, studying Ryan for trickery. The blood from Markus' body taints the air with death. Gripping Melody's wrists in one hand, I cut the binds there, reaching up to cut the one at her neck. I feel him come at me but cutting her down is worth the blade scorching my ribs as it punctures my lung. The pain is extreme but not as agonising as the fact my kid brother just stabbed me.

I collapse to the floor, Melody landing in a heap on top of me, arousing from her semi-conscious state. The bucket tips and spills its freezing contents to the floor. She's being pulled from me. I'm losing her, losing everything. I can't bear to watch what we built burn. I can't crawl around in the ashes fighting to put out the embers threatening to change me irrevocably. I won't survive her death at his hand, if I survive at all. The ooze of my warm blood saturates my shirt. I can't believe this is how I'm losing her. She's mine. I'm the creator of nightmares yet here I am living my own. My world is ending right in front of me and at the hands of the only other person I loved my whole life.

They say you know when you meet the one. Melody impacted me so forcibly, she tattooed her soul onto mine and I can't let my darkness take her from the world. He's my responsibility. I let him shape me into what I am. I should have seen through the smokescreen.

I need her to wake up. I need her to fight but she can't. Damn, my sun is betraying me, her light fading into the shadows of my brother's demons. How did I allow him to become this far gone?

"Did I fuck you up this bad?" I choke out, the blood coming up my throat; that's a real bad sign. I have to keep asking myself if this is real, if this scene is actually happening. I was trying to grapple with the air to fill my lungs.

He appears over me, shaking his head. "You just aren't getting it, Blake. You murdering and treating people like meat sacks could fuck up any sibling."

My breath wheezes in and out of me in a whistle. "Listing my sins can't redeem you of yours, Ry."

His teeth grind together. "I don't want to be redeemed, you're missing the point! You didn't do anything. I was born this way. I have always felt a sense of incurable and absolute restlessness and boredom in my own skin. Everyone around me was different to me but the same as each other. You are all an undifferentiated mass of weakness ruled by love and loyalty. I never understood but wanted to govern." He rolls his neck, inhales through his teeth, the sound hissing into the room. I see a flicker of movement from Melody but I don't want to draw his attention to it. I need to keep him talking so she can get out.

"Did my love for you not mean anything? I'm your brother."

His head tilts to the side as he studies me with pity. "I like that you love me and I used it. I craved manipulation. Changing someone's life is a powerful thing. Watching people unravel, pushing them so far into my depravity, making them question if it's their own is an insatiable need. I have an appetite for harm, and I only really feel like I exist when I'm superior. The only thing that drives me is possessing and destroying others inside and out, body and soul. I want to strip them bare so they're empty like me." He kicks at my legs. "You should be thanking me, Blake, for putting you out of your misery. I want to watch Mel's face as the last breath leaves your lungs. I want her to think you killed her parents."

I'm crying for the first time in countless years. Tears burn a trail down my cheeks. My brother was just an illusion. This person standing over me is not of this world. He is the definition of evil. I assumed Markus had hired another guy as well as me when I entered the house that night to find the massacre. I was just leaving when she walked in.

"You killed them?"

My life is diminishing, white vapour clouding my eyesight.

"I was just going to come and watch you. I arrived the night before and couldn't resist introducing myself as a friend of Mel's just visiting the area and they were so hospitable, inviting me to stay for dinner." He grins over at Markus' corpse practically in the same position as her mother's.

"I'm sorry. Oh God, I'm sorry, Blake." Melody's cries pierce the air. I hear the entry, the swoosh of the air against the blade, the hiccup sound as it plunders in. "Argh, I'm sorry! God forgive me." Her strangled screams are more agonising than the night she found her parents.

Ryan's utter disbelief shows all over his face. She was guided by an invisible force giving her strength because the blade goes all the way through his back, the tip appearing through his stomach. He falls forward, tipping to the side, to land with a thud beside me. Black orbs of a soulless boy look back at me. No matter how much my brain tells me the brother I loved was never even in here, my heart still bleeds as I watch him die. Puffs of air in short sharp bursts escape his lips before he stills. No movement. Nothing. I succumb to beckoning sleep pulling me under.

Chapter 40

Moving on

Melody

BLAKE WAS IN A COMA for six weeks; internal injuries nearly took his life. I had nearly taken a life with my own two hands. Ryan needed to die. He was put together like us but is the furthest thing from human. He played the role, deceived, manipulated and corrupted souls. He is the master of sin, wielded by the devil's hands but I'm not God. I didn't get to decide his fate. Once they found a heartbeat, they took away his life, imprisoning him in a hospital for the clinically insane. He took everything from me and although Blake didn't kill my parents, he still came to my house to do just that. How can I let myself

empathy

be with someone capable of that? How can I love him so deeply that I want to curl up and die from the ache of not being with him?

I waited by his bedside day in day out for him to wake up. Six weeks of not knowing. You can do a lot in six weeks. Quitting college. Investing in the newspaper company. Having that house demolished; there was no way I could keep it after so much darkness took place there. I'll keep the land, let it grow wild and give it back to nature.

Starting over is a scary prospect but one I need. I kept what I learned about Blake a secret which was an internal battle with my morals. My love for him overpowered them. He has been a victim in such a big way. It doesn't excuse him of his sins but I won't divulge them either. I'll just try and forget I ever came to that town. I'll ignore the suffocating vice wrapped around my ever shrinking heart and try to live. Try to move on.

Three weeks have passed since I left him in the hospital and my mind can't concentrate on Sean as he orders our coffees. He came to see me about Ryan. Told me things I wished he hadn't. It was by Ryan's hand that Sean ended up in front of the car that nearly took his life. He's fully recovered health wise, but the emotional scars are imprinted on him, just like they are on me.

"So you went to stay with your ex?" His raised brow is playfully accusing.

I take my coffee from his hand. "It's not like that. I just needed some normalcy. He offers me that." I'd spent a week with Zane after leaving Blake awake in the hospital. I needed his comfort.

We walk from the shop; the cooler nights are a welcome reprieve from the humidity of the passing heatwave.

"You're the strongest person I know, Mel. I don't know how you survive. I struggle to get out of bed every day. I feel so betrayed by myself, by my own inability to not see the wicked amongst the good."

I slip my hand into his. "I'm dying inside little by little. I have days when I think I conquered the war he created in me but I'm still fighting every day to find peace. He took so much from me but he didn't break me completely like he wanted. I'm breathing, I'm living. I fought too hard to save my life to let him defeat me without even being here. He's gone Sean."

We make it back to my new apartment, my footing stalling when a broken Blake is sitting on the floor, his back against my front door. His rises to meet me.

"Oh, this is embarrassing. I thought you just weren't opening the door. I've been talking to myself."

My neighbor's door opens, she's cuddling her cat, her hair in rollers. "I tried to tell him and then threatened to call the police but he said he is the police and he showed me a badge and everything. That must be how he made it past the front desk."

"Thanks, Linda," I murmur, waving her in to her apartment. I give my keys to Sean and tell him to wait inside. He nervously eyes Blake before complying.

"What are you doing here? How did you even find me?"

He reaches into his pocket, pulling out his phone. "GPS."

Of course he would hack my GPS.

It hurts to even look at him. My heart is a stampede of wild horses, their stomps echoing through me, making every hair rise from the surface of my skin. "I can't do this, Blake. Say what you need to and leave."

He shakes his head. "I'm not leaving." I open my mouth to reply but he holds up his hand to mute me. "When the sun sets, you can't hold on to the dying light as the darkening shadow approaches. You either hide from it or become it. I can't make excuses, you know them all anyway. I'm not a perfect person, not good enough for you by a long shot. I have done some horrible shit and witnessed evil in its truest form but you awoke a side of me I didn't know existed anymore. You reassembled a part of me I thought disintegrated into dust. You gave me a reason to seek out the soul that once lived here." He thumps his fist against his chest. "The heart that once wasn't so fucking cold and..." His eyes drop to my feet. "Lonely, Mel. God, it's a lonely cold place to be. Locked inside my head. The anger. The regret. I didn't expect you. I didn't know I was capable of loving you. I didn't realise amongst the beckoning night the sun can rise again, chase out the darkness, teach the damned to be less lonely, to find love so empowering it makes everything in your life before it obliterate."

Tears burn a trail down my cheeks, igniting a fire beneath them. I need to wake up.

empathy

"I don't know who I am without you. I'm sinking, drowning in the truth of everything that passed. I loved him, Mel. I raised and killed for him and it was all a game. He was pulling me like a rubber band to see how far he could stretch me before I snapped."

He's breaking right in front of me. I could reach out and reconstruct the soul fraying into tethers with nothing to latch onto. I could offer him my heart to bleed into, letting my pulse power us both. He was choking but I could breathe for him, if I could forgive myself for loving him. It still felt like a betrayal to my parents. He wasn't their killer but he could have been.

"You absorbed my soul, Puya, and I don't want it back. I want to be the pulse in you. I miss you, it's killing me. I'm dying without you. I don't want to exist in a world where you're not loving me."

That's the thing. It doesn't matter about anything else. The only thing that matters is that I love him and I can't stop. He owns me and I own him.

Epilogue

8 years later

8 years later

Blake

"DADDY...DADDY!"

Every single day this is how she wakes me up. Her little feet trample over my calves as she clumsily climbs over my body to sit on my shoulders and whisper in my ear despite the shouting not seconds before.

"Guess what?" Her hushed little breath warms my ear.

"What?" I grumble into the pillow

"Aunt Ruth is here and she said she's sending the boys up here in ten minutes if you're not up and dressed."

Damn that witch of a sister of mine. It took a couple of years but the bond with my sisters and father was one built on tragedy, guilt and lost time made up tenfold by unconditional acceptance and love.

"The boys? Nooooo please not the boys."

The boys are my nephews and they, unlike my little angel, wouldn't just trample my calves, they would dive bomb me until I fell from the bed.

Her giggles sound through the room, igniting light in me I never knew I could harbor. When Melody fell into my arms at her apartment, she never left them. I put a ring on her finger a month later and this little cherub now tracing the ink of her name, Cereus, over my shoulder came a year later.

We grew and learned, coped and breathed together. Ryan changed us both for the worst but we changed each other for the better. Fate entwined us and although the devil led me down many sinful paths, God could be the only reason I met Melody. She was a saint sent to save me and she did. We survived, I awoke. I feel. I love. I have empathy.

10 Years Later than that

Ryan

EIGHTEEN YEARS OF BEING TRAPPED inside a place full of people so broken, manipulation is like child's play. Nurses working long hours on poor money with husbands not showing them interest ate me up when I arrived. The funny thing is, we're called the insane ones yet how crazy do you have to be to yearn for someone like me? But they do. This face can melt the panties off a nun. Who's the broken one, people?

Melody played roles in here she didn't know about. I'm still a little bitter how things played out in the end. See, when I claim someone they stay in me forever, an obsession if you like. They live in my skin, in the blood that pumps through my veins. I don't like losing and that was exactly what it felt like when she plunged that knife in me.

My mind relives everything that happened; killing her parents,

empathy

bashing that cunting vermin's head in who called me a punk ass faggot when I passed him in the alley behind Club Blue. Clive and the filthy whores from Club Nine, the blood flowing from them in rivers of wine. Mmmm, breaking Sean. He was in love with me and dreamed about me taking him. I watched his elation when I told him I wanted him too, then took him so brutally with my fist he cried and squealed like a baby pig being strangled. I offered to walk him home afterwards because he was too sore to sit in the seat of my car. He was so upset with himself for not being able to handle my type of sexual needs, repeatedly apologising to me. How pathetic. It was almost no fun playing with him; I prefer a stronger mind. The disbelief and fear that flitted across his face when I shoved him into the oncoming traffic is a memory I savor though. I let those memories get me through this pit stop in my life.

They think they cure you but this is me, no matter how many doctors, how much medication, they can't cure someone who isn't ill. I'm not ill. I didn't break. I was never whole to begin with.

"Are you ready to start your new life, Ryan? You're about to become a part of the world again, be an upstanding civilian and then in a year you won't even have to come to visit me." My psychiatrist beams.

"Live amongst the normal people?" I quipped.

"You're normal Ryan." God how wrong he is.

I slip on my jacket and tug down the picture that plays host to dissolute dreams. Something they tried to hide from me but only goaded me to play the recovered patient.

My lovely niece, a perfect mix of Melody and Blake.

My voice replies, "I'm ready." My mind is saying, "I'm not normal. I don't feel. I don't love.

I don't have empathy."

The End

Keep reading for a look at upcoming releases

The People who make it all happen.

Ker Dukey – Author
Website - www.kerdukey.com/
Follow me here
https://www.facebook.com/KerDukeyauthor?ref_type=bookmark
https://twitter.com/KerDukeyauthor

Editor - Kyra Lennon
http://www.kyralennon.com/

Formatter – Champagne Formats
https://www.facebook.com/ChampagneFormats

Cover model – Collin Atkins
https://www.facebook.com/bookcollin

Photographer – Clyph Unbounded-By Words
www.unboundedbywords.com

Cover design – Cover it designs
www.coveritdesigns.net

Publicist - Concierge Literary Promotions
Clpromotionsky.net

Acknowledgments

This book wouldn't have been possible without the amazing support I receive so I would like to take a moment to thank a few people.

My family who sacrifice time with me so I can spend half my life in the writing cave, living the life's of many characters to bring you these stories. Thank you to my amazing street team who pimp me hard through pure passion for my books. Your dedication, loyalty and love, means the world to me. My incredible beta readers who drop everything to read my work and encourage and support me to keep writing. Michelle McGinty, Vikki Ryan, Vicki Leaf, Kristin Bairos, Terrie Arasin and Jillian Crouson Toth. I love you girls so much, your friendship above everything else is selfless and loyal thank you. My other half, Dawn Stancil aka D.H.Sidebottom! She is a lifeline I would drown in this market without. She is an incredible author who I look up to and who inspires me but she is also an amazing woman. Life likes to kick her around but that woman gets back up and shows it the middle finger. She is a strong, beautiful, loving friend who I cherish. Thank you to all the incredible blogs that support me. To all the authors who inspire me. Thank you to my amazing editor and friend Kyra! My incredible formatter Stacey, who always makes room for me on her busy schedule. This book is at its best because of you two. Thank you to the beautiful, Collin for gracing my cover and his super talented photographer, Clyph for capturing a perfect shot. Cover it designs for making it into the perfect cover. Thanks to my publicists and friends Judi and Kiki and my wonderful friend and hard worker at pimping my butt! Crystal Solis, I love these women hard.

Sneak peek at upcoming works.

Facade

A Dark NA Romance erotica

D.H SIDEBOTTOM & KER DUKEY

Blurb and prolgue

You meet someone. You date. You fall in love. You marry.

The four simple rules of love….

Wrong! I'm getting married but I'd never met him before now, never dated him, never fell in love. I have no access to the memories of the most magical time of anyone's life.

My mind won't allow me to evoke the past, I can't remember those simple stages to lead me to the fourth.

I can't comprehend why I would have ever wanted to marry someone like Dante. I should never have passed the first stage, although, I may have seen him through the eyes of the woman I once was, this me that lives, breathes here now, can't understand how we made it to the next stage.

I'm not sure, without memories, how I know that this voice inside me, telling me I would never have chosen him, speaks some truth, I just know. He's controlling, arrogant, callous and violent, and utterly hell bent on humiliating and degrading me – Like watching me falter, watching me struggle to comply and be the woman he asked to marry, powers him- as though he wants to break me piece by piece. Fiber by fiber. Until all that's here is the shell he created from a soul that I once owned.

Now my memories are slowly returning. And they show me a completely different side to meeting him. Our dates, falling in love. The Dante haunting me in the shadows of my mind is loving, gentle and utterly enamored with me, nothing like the man with me now.

And this is what taunts me. My tender lover turned into a debauched, cruel sadist who is determined to consume my life, destroy my mind and murder my spirit.

I am, Star, and just like with some stars in the sky, the light you see is an echo, a façade, I am already gone

I am a no one.

Especially to him. To him I am the dark in his desires, the corrupt in his depravity.

The sin in his immorality.

Prologue
Proposal

Star

The sun heated my skin, its rays licking over me, branding me in its golden glow and warming my already sensitive body. The smell of lotion was intoxicating as firm familiar hands I craved to have touch me rubbed over contours of my body, rough fingers sliding along every inch of me. White sand and clear blue ocean as far as the eye could see relaxed me further.

This is what we needed, we both worked too hard, we never indulged or took time for just us two.

We lived out one of his fantasies last night, him taking me in the open where anyone could be watching; although making love under the blue hue of the moonlight, on a secluded beach where he'd created a romantic bed of rose petals wasn't exactly where we could be caught. But it was still the most memorial night of my life and hopefully his too.

I looked down to the twinkling diamond of my engagement ring and smiled contentedly. He had completely taken me off guard last

empathy

night.

The memory played over, letting me relive the most magical proposal I could have asked for. Him pushing his body to join with mine before stilling when he was fully sheathed inside the warmth of my body. His soft gaze captured mine, his eyes glimmering with a thousand emotions before murmuring, "You were created to complete my soul and mine yours. When the sun sets and rises every day from this day forward we will be forever entwined. I promise I'll give you everything, friendship..." He peppered my face in kisses, his soft lips burying me in his love. "...Passion..." he thrust deeply, his hips pressing against mine, making me moan out. "...Babies with my brains and your looks." He smiled cheekily, rubbing one hand over my stomach.

I gasped slapping his shoulder which made him twitch deliciously inside me. I wanted to beg him to move, he was filling me up completely but not moving. Yet, his words made my heart thud and my mind race with the intensity I could feel seeping from him, their honesty drenching me in the truth of his promise.

"I'll support your dreams and live to make them come true." His eyes darkened, his gaze never leaving mine as his eyes hypnotised me. "I'll make every fantasy fulfilled" His hand cupped my face, the softness of his palm both comforting and exciting. "I'll protect you, honour you and God, love you more than anything."

My eyes were glassy, I couldn't stop the tears from forming. He continued as his voice dropped in tone, his brow furrowed like he was concentrating, reminiscing. "I always felt connected to you, as if a string from my soul was tethered to yours."

His hand looped a thread around my ring finger. The tears spilled free when I noticed the other end was looped around his own finger, a platinum band with a huge diamond sat on the end of his chunky finger. He tilted his hand, making the ring flow free down the thread until it looped onto mine. I choked on a happy sob. "Promise never to leave me, to never love another man. Promise to be my wife, promise to complete us?"

I couldn't speak I wrapped my arms around him tightly, bringing his head down to the crease of my neck as I nuzzled into his. My legs wrapped firmly around his waist as I dug the heels of my feet into his ass, urging and begging him to move.

His laugh resonating against my skin. "Is that a yes?" His head lifted to look into my eyes.

I swallowed and inhaled, catching the breath I needed to breathe out again. "I can't promise I will never love another man." I whispered against his ear. His body stilled, he wasn't even breathing. I quickly continued before I ruined the moment and he passed out from lack of oxygen. "If he looks like you." His eyes widened. "And calls me mommy, I will love him."

His breath rushed out of him, warming my lips. "Promise me!" He demanded with a thrust of his hips. His full length glided against my inner walls, eliciting pleasure into my core. "Promise me," he growled in frustration as his body covered every part of mine.

"I promise, I promise!" I cried out as he took me over the edge, onwards to make a start on the promises we both made…

Add to your goodreads list
https://www.goodreads.com/book/show/22293515-facade?ac=1

The Decimation of Mae

by D.H Sidebottom

available now

Blurb

The Devil visited me three times in my life; albeit, my short life. Not in the physical sense, you must understand, but very much literally.

He was persistent, resolute and tenacious. His ruthless greed to annihilate me was utterly disturbing. I am sure if he had hierarchy, the man at the top would have dragged his arse into Hell's prison for his unscrupulous methods.

I was just fifteen when I first became aware of what he was capable of. This initial taste of him set the playing field for how my life was to be lived – for want of a better word.

He mocked me, showed me mercilessly how he played the game and how he liked to cheat at said game. He ridiculed and taunted me until, six months later, he won and took something of so much importance from me that I would never be the same again.

His second visit was, in my eyes, so much more cruel and heartless. I know we're talking about the Devil here, and yes, you have a right to say he had no heart but even then, even when I was so utterly broken, I begged to differ and hoped – no, prayed – that somewhere deep in the caverns of his black, tortured soul there was something that beat and confused his emotions once in a while.

The third visit was somewhat different than the other two. He tried, and at first succeeded to bring me to my knees once and for all, but then something happened. God finally intervened and altered Satan's intention; he sent hope and morphed the Devil's minion into an Angel, hoping to break and shatter the anguish and suffering. He gave the ability for me to feel pleasure in pain, order in the chaos and light in the darkness.

But in giving me a reprieve, he also gave me something that would finally and ultimately obliterate me. He gave me the capability to love, therefore giving me the ability to be destroyed.

And Satan made sure that I was destroyed. Cruelly, viciously and sadistically.

I am Mae Swift, and this is the story of my decimation.

Coming November 2014

Nobody Knows

by Kyra Lennon

Blurb

It's not easy being friends with rising rock stars - especially when you're the glue that holds them together.

Razes Hell has taken off in the charts, and Ellie can't believe her childhood friends, Drew and Jason Brooks, are on TV and drawing crowds after years spent playing in dodgy bars. From obscurity to overnight success, Ellie soon realises life in the public eye isn't all it's cracked up to be as dark secrets become headline news and old conflicts are re-ignited. When a fake feud meant to boost the band's popularity threatens to rip the boys apart for real, Ellie finds herself torn – a position which only gets more uncomfortable when her loyalty to Jason collides with her blossoming relationship with Drew.

Nobody knows how deep their issues run; nobody but Ellie. With friendship, a music career and a new love on the line, can Ellie keep their tangled pasts from ruining their futures?

https://www.goodreads.com/book/show/22839584-nobody-knows

Made in the USA
Charleston, SC
31 August 2014